# Mariposilla

# Mariposilla

Mary Stewart Daggett

MINT EDITIONS

*Mariposilla* was first published in 1896.

This edition published by Mint Editions 2021.

ISBN 9781513279152 | E ISBN 9781513279367

Published by Mint Editions®

MINT
EDITIONS

minteditionbooks.com

Publishing Director: Jennifer Newens
Design & Production: Rachel Lopez Metzger
Project Manager: Micaela Clark
Typesetting: Westchester Publishing Services

# Contents

# I

When I abandoned the home of my girlhood, and took my delicate child to California, I started upon the journey goaded only by apathetic hopes, sustained only by the desperation of despair.

Marjorie was my all, and I could no longer endure the tension of her gradual decline. As I watched her fade away, I realized that my closest friends were becoming reconciled to my bereavement, with the philosophical fortitude of spectators. When I was coolly advised "not to sacrifice pecuniary interests for the sentiment of a hopeless experiment," an outraged love grew strong and defiant. The calculating counsel, so cruel and unexpected, strengthened, at last, the timid resolution. Even the silent walls of my house oppressed, while an absolute hatred of the machinery of life seized my tired soul. I determined to be free at any price. Fresh courage entered my life, and impelled me to remove, without a pang, most cherished household gods. My relief was immoderate when everything was gone. Then I experienced for the first time in years the sweet exhilaration that welcomes, breathlessly, a change. In my dreams I had apparitions of purple mountains, and long quiet days purified with sunshine. Suddenly, into my sad life there came new hope, kindled, it seemed, from the very ashes of an abortive past.

Before I realized the initial steps of my undertaking, anticipated perplexities had been absorbed by the novel conditions of our journey. Four days away from the old home and New York found me happier than for months, when I saw for the first time a flush upon the pallid cheeks of my child, the faintest reflection of the coveted boon I sought.

A fresh excitement made me strong for each new duty. The present at last held all that I craved. When I watched my child among her pillows, so much better that she prattled of great plans to be carried out on the far away Coast, I loved even then the land. To see the little one sleep, and watch for her awakening among the great quiet mountains, was to my heart an ecstasy. "Dear Mamma," she cried, clasping her thin hands as the train clambered close to the silent monarchs of the West, "I want to touch they!"

"Yes, sweetheart," I said; "When Marjorie is strong and well, she shall not only touch the dear mountains, but she shall crawl into their very arms! Mamma will take her into the beautiful cañons, where little streams always sing to the tall ferns; we shall have a picnic, and perhaps the fairies will come! When my little girl sees the Fairy Queen she can ask for a boon, like Mabel in the song. Perhaps the Queen will say: 'So this is little Marjorie, who came all the way from New York to see us? Marjorie is a good child, and was very patient during her long journey. She took her bitter medicine bravely, and now she must be rewarded. What shall be done for her, my Fairies?'

"Then perhaps one kind fairy may say, 'Her cheeks must grow pink like a La France rose'; and another, 'Her limbs must grow strong like a perfect tree'; and a third, 'Her eyes must be bright like the stars, and she must soon be well, and as happy as she is pretty.'"

Thus I romanced to my patient child, snatching an inspiration from every mile that drove us into the far country.

When we entered the wide, trackless desert—the home of distorted yuccas, which stretched gaunt arms to the cloudless sky, like hopeless criminals doomed to the intermediate wastes of purgatory—I knew that the "Happy Valley" lay beyond. Then my child was sleeping for long hours at a time; nor did she awaken until the last yucca had vanished from the desert's edge; then she opened her eyes in Wonderland! For the overland train had completed its conquest. The great mountain chains had been passed over in safety, while far behind, fields of snow and shrieking blasts were forgotten, as we glided peacefully into the beautiful Valley of San Gabriel, that Pet Marjorie might live.

Our long journey was ended. We could rest, although not perfectly until after leaving the pleasant hotel known as the East San Gabriel, when I hoped to find in the old Spanish home of the Doña Maria Del Valle the coveted seclusion of which I had dreamed.

From the beginning of our journey, everyone had been interested in Marjorie.

I soon found myself accepting small attentions from sympathetic strangers as naturally as I would have accepted, a few weeks before, the favors of old friends.

It thus happened that I first heard of the Doña Maria Del Valle, through a lady and her son with whom I traveled. "A most perfect place for Pet Marjorie would be with the Doña Maria Del Valle," Mrs. Sanderson had told me, shortly after our arrival in San Gabriel, when I inquired of all for a home that would shelter us for at least a year. Marjorie must not live in a hotel, exposed to the constant excitement of robust children and irresponsible strangers.

Besides, I desired to try not only the winter of Southern California, but the long, unimpassioned summer, so conducive to the restoration of the delicate.

My new friend had spent the previous season in San Gabriel; she was familiar with the locality, and offered at once to intercede in our behalf with the Doña Maria Del Valle. When she told, in her captivating way, of the quaint, picturesque Spanish home, I could content myself with no other retreat, and begged that the preliminary arrangements might be made at once. From the first moment of our acquaintance, Mrs. Sanderson's attentions had been agreeable. As soon as we arrived at the hotel she was perfectly at home. Every one hastened to serve her, and I perceived that she was an acknowledged authority wherever she went. My mind was not then equal to the analysis of character. I was unsuspicious and willing to believe in the assumed qualities of those about me. It was enough that my child was improving hourly in health, and that I had found a congenial and sympathetic companion in my extremity.

Now that I have undertaken a story in which Mrs. Sanderson and her son Sidney so conspicuously figure, I feel compelled to review carefully my early and subsequent impressions of both, in order that the events of our short and memorable acquaintance may be readily understood.

Doubtless my estimate of entire strangers would have been different under less intense circumstances; but, at that time, any one who appeared interested in my child was at once my friend—not only the conspicuous and influential, but the humble and uncultivated, as well. Looking back over those trying weeks, I now remember hosts of delicate attentions dispensed by the unpretentious, that at the time were hardly realized, owing to the effusive ostentations of the Sandersons.

Since I have studied carefully the events which followed rapidly from the beginning of our acquaintance, I am certain that neither Marjorie nor myself would have received the slightest notice from either Mrs. Sanderson or her son, had we failed in their selfish entertainment. My little girl, beautiful and bright, unconsciously stole into the coldest hearts; but I know now that it was not her delicate frame, nor the pathos of a defrauded childhood that won the devotion of Mrs. Sanderson. It was simply that Marjorie was an additional amusement, an additional effect, enlivening the small court which the lady invariably held. The capricious woman petted the child only for entertainment. A thoroughbred dog, or a kitten, could have won her interest as successfully, had her passing mood been favorable to their antics. Her fancy for myself was equally selfish. I was young enough to interest her son, and from the first she evidently regarded me as a convenient and suitable companion for the winter. I learned afterwards that Mrs. Sanderson was notoriously fond of young widows. She treated them with unusual favor in view of eventual schemes which she generally worked. Her only idea of life was entertainment, and, in order to satisfy her thirst for novelty, she had always chosen pretty widows to expand her power and promote her individual caprices. Unincumbered by the unreasonable demands of a husband, she regarded a pathetic young widow a most desirable companion; always securing, if possible, a fresh one for the nucleus of her social experiments.

Why I should have submitted to this woman's patronage, I can not understand. My only excuse is the recollection of an unsuspicious joy, that came like new life into my soul. Marjorie was getting well! and there was no one who understood my happiness like Mrs. Sanderson. It never occurred to me to doubt her sincerity. That she was often haughty and disagreeable to others I saw, but for me she had only indulgence and delicate sympathy. Under calming climatic influences my pagan intuitions grew hourly. Beneath the lights and shadows of the prophetic mountains, analytical tendencies ceased. Possibly my creeds became unorthodox, but they expanded cheerfully each day, that they might hold more of God's harmonious universe and less of man's deformity.

I believed afresh in universal philanthropy. The sweet lethargic days were satisfying; I had no desire to analyze the motives of my associates.

I was no longer interested in attenuated studies of character. The Book of Nature, and the literal tales of "Mother Goose" now constituted my library. For the present, the Wise Men of Athens were no wiser than the man who so successfully evaded the consequences of the "bramble bush." Now that my child had been given back to me, no unnecessary suspicions disturbed my credulous content. I had been tired so long, that to rest, at last, necessarily developed passive conditions over which I had but languid control.

Mrs. Sanderson, crossing my path at this particular time, appeared to be the very person to stimulate my reviving interest in life, and I accepted eagerly and without analysis the friendship she offered.

From the first, I had been fascinated by her alertness. Unconsciously, I felt indebted to her for my renewed fortunes. It was not until long afterward that I discovered how very little she really did for me, or for anyone else, when she appeared to be doing so much. She always assumed the leadership of social affairs so cleverly, that to have questioned her right would have proved fatal to the individual. It was impossible to resist her personality when she chose to be engaging.

She was tall and slender, with the established slenderness that emphasizes distinction at forty-five, when plump women often exhibit the ripeness of decay.

In a word, Mrs. Sanderson eclipsed completely her feminine contemporaries, often exciting jealous antagonisms.

The lady's superior preservation was at times exasperating, and her scornful indifference to topics usually interesting to middle life disconcerted and annoyed domestic women of her own age. Her infirmities she heroically concealed, and was never surprised into the acknowledgement of a physical weakness. The chronic afflictions of other women never moved her to sympathetic confidences. In fact, she avoided systematically the society of older women, while she ingratiated herself irresistibly with young people of both sexes.

For these reasons, Mrs. Sanderson was frequently disliked, but as few dared to oppose her openly, her sway always grew to be absolute.

# II

Mrs. Sanderson, at the various stations of her social pilgrimage, had managed to create fresh enthusiasms for every shrine. Each year found her alert, substituting new images for those cast down, and, withal, grading so ingeniously the declivities of time, that the world failed to detect the skillful engineering, because for her there had been none of those abrupt drops so disastrous to the grace of womanhood.

She was always in sympathy with the age. For this reason she was perpetually surrounded by young people, who referred to her upon all questions, accepting her decree as preëminent.

Her distinguished bearing and captivating manners were so infectious that, before she had been in San Gabriel a week, she was the recognized authority of the hotel.

It was suicidal to one's standing with a laundress to advocate the doctrines of unfluted linen, contrary to the opinion of Mrs. Sanderson. Even the non-emotional Wing Lee replied to my entreaty "to handle less roughly Marjorie's frocks": "High tone lady *she* muchey likey my washey! my starchey!" I felt the propriety of the rebuke when Mrs. Sanderson at that moment sauntered past my door.

Having established her position, even in the estimation of the domestics and Celestials, it is not surprising that at the end of two weeks she was widely known in the district of San Gabriel. Devoutly feared by the usual social barometers of the hotel, adored by all on whom she smiled, and hated by the unfortunate few ostracized from her favor, she seemed the sun of the San Gabriel social system, compelling Sidney and every one about her to reflect modestly the capricious beams she magnanimously bestowed. In the meantime, a marvelous change had taken place in the bare apartments that, up to the present time, had not been distinguished as the choice of a popular leader. The rooms were no longer suggestive of the fluctuating tourist, but suddenly became rich in abiding personality and comfort.

It was observable that the obsequious housekeeper had rifled other apartments, and that couches and easy chairs had materialized with a due conformity to the prolific climate.

The formerly obtrusive white walls soon grew companionable, as pictures, draperies, Japanese plaques, and characteristic Indian baskets sprouted upon them each night. In all directions were strewn evidences of travel and refinement.

In the bepillowed alcove a dainty tea table invited the five o'clock teabibbers of the circle elect, while a piano and stringed instruments allured the musical, and always the young.

More noticeable, however, than all else in the rooms was the display of attractive photographs, indicating for the Sandersons a large and distinguished acquaintance of beautiful women.

"Sid's sweethearts!" the mother said playfully, to the girls who questioned her about the rival beauties, and when a pert miss bravely intimated that young Sanderson must be "a kind of a Blue Beard," the lady good-naturedly replied: "Oh, yes, Sid is terribly fickle. Most of the dear ones have been beheaded long ago, and now the naughty boy is only in love with his mother."

At the same time, we noticed that the face of one beautiful girl was repeated many times in the collection, and inferred that this particular beauty still found favor.

The son was noncommittal. He submitted indifferently to the attentions of the various young women who thronged his mother's rooms, yet more often appeared bored than entertained.

Had I met Sidney away from his clever relative, I am certain I would never have honored him with my acquaintance; but from the first his mother compelled me, as well as her entire circle of friends, to accept the young man at her estimate. Sidney Sanderson was undoubtedly a striking development of his type; but foolish indulgence, a naturally indolent and unsympathetic disposition—together with certain disreputable vices, had made him totally unworthy of the consideration he received. About his full, blond physique there was a blasé indifference which unfortunately very often fascinates young girls. Yet, without his mother, the young man would have found it difficult to retain social approbation. Deprived of her shielding expedients, his dissipations would have become notorious, his gentlemanly pretensions questioned.

Away from her far-reaching influence, her vigilant contrivance and conquering resources, he would not have been long courted or extolled.

The usual unhappy demand for young men would doubtless have insured, for a time, his toleration about the hotel, but his position would have been different. He would have been openly criticised, and perhaps denounced, unprotected by his mother's popularity.

As it was, no one dared to hint an unfavorable judgment on the son of the gifted mother who put words into his mouth and characteristics to his account, which, in reminiscent moods, must have embarrassed him.

Mrs. Sanderson approved, or withered instantly, our plans, although she never neglected to refer with the sweetest subserviency to her son. "Ask Sid," she would say; "I dare say he will think it quite the thing for us all, but his judgments are so much quieter than mine, that he is best to consult." Thus she constituted her self-instructed oracle a paramount authority.

I am still fascinated with the recollections of this wily woman. Her ability to deceive captivates me now, as, in the beginning of our acquaintanceship, it enthralled my reason and silenced my prejudices.

Not satisfied with posing her son before the young and unthinking as a model of refinement, endowed with the intrinsic qualities of manhood, his intellectual upheavals were often depicted in side talk, with celebrities. Once with maternal discretion as fine as it was impertinent, she told our latest nervously prostrated authoress, who was enjoying a cup of tea in the alcove, about her boy's passion for old books. "Sidney's library is his one extravagance," she confided, sweetly. Then, with unblushing assurance, she told how her son's intellectual indulgence had cost her an orange ranch; yet, owing to the extremely moral character of the fad, she had grown resigned. Only once had she ventured a remonstrance—when a fabulous sum was paid for an atrocious old Dante, too absolutely filthy for any one but a connoisseur. Of course, she knew she was uncultivated, but she preferred her books fresh and clean, with attractive covers. However, there were compensations with every trial, and Sid's veneration for antiquities might still prove a blessing, as she herself would some day be sufficiently antique to justify his supreme devotion.

Thus the woman audaciously chattered, advertising fearlessly the bogus literary tastes of her son.

If we questioned Sidney's phenomenal reticence upon subjects so near his heart, for convenient reasons all appeared willing to accept the mother's version of the unexplored country where gold abounded—and still waters ran to a depth unparalleled.

Now that the scales have fallen from my eyes, I have spare justification for this woman, for so many weeks my daily companion. Even a mother's desperation can not excuse her conduct, although it may possibly moderate its enormity in the eyes of those who have sought to shield with ornate falsehood an unworthy child. With the woman's clear perception, she must have known more certainly than all others the fullest truth concerning her son. She could not be blind to his aimless life, his selfish nature, his depraved, ill-controlled passions. Yet, with all her superior knowledge of the risk, she deemed it her right to supplement her boy's deficiencies by chimerical attractions, sheltering him, if possible, to the end, beneath the decencies and refinements of society.

Without his mother in the breach, Sidney Sanderson would undoubtedly have been publicly disgraced many times, for he was not a clever rogue. Yet, only once, to my knowledge, did his disreputable conduct appear in print, and even then the mother proved herself equal to the dastardly emergencies of the scandal.

The affair occurred in one of the quick-grown Western cities in which the Sandersons were financially interested. They lived in the place for a number of months, and were soon the center of the fashionable! questionable! mushroom! set of the town. I had the story from an eye witness of the unique local travesty, which, together with my personal knowledge of the leading lady's adaptation for her part, enabled me to readily imagine the dramatic force of the situation.

It was simple to see a group of fair gossipers, suspending instantly the bold assertions of the moment, when the tall, gracious, masterful Mrs. Sanderson appeared among them, holding in her beautiful jeweled hands the daily paper. Still easier to fancy the incredulous expressions, followed by eager devotion to fancy work, when the lady deliberately seated herself in the cosy corner of the hotel corridor and read, unflinchingly, a long, scandalous article, replete with stinging invective, which everyone knew applied to but one man, and that man her son. I could fancy the woman asking insolently, at the close of her desperate performance, if any one could locate the "Blond Lothario" of the sensation, feeling absolutely sure that no voice would answer.

Such was Mrs. Sanderson's nerve, such her diabolical vigor. So strong were her restraining influences, and so unflinching her power, that none of the social squad dared to confront her with her lie. It was not until weeks afterwards, when both mother and son had left the town, that tongues were loosened and restricted gossips happy.

# III

It has appeared wise to relate at once my warranted impression of Mrs. Sanderson. Having failed so completely in the early part of our intimacy to penetrate her character, I offer the reader an advantage; and that the events which follow may be better understood, I have endeavored to make plain her supreme selfishness.

As previously stated, it was she who first told me about the home of the Del Valles. The year before, she had gone to the ranch in quest of the exquisite drawn work, done upon the finest linen, for which the Doña Maria was famous; and so charmed had the lady been with the recollection of the picturesque visit, that she hastened, upon her return to San Gabriel, to renew the acquaintance.

She was surprised to find the family much less prosperous than formerly, and the ranch mortgaged for almost its value. The proud Doña Maria told her, with quiet tears, how all was wrong; how her grandnephew Arturo had gone to Old Mexico to renew, if possible, the failing fortunes of his family, while upon her, assisted by an idle Mexican, had fallen the sole responsibility of the ranch; how it was impossible not to neglect many things now that Arturo was gone, for her aged mother was again bad with the old spells, and soon must make a great care. But most deplorable of all, her little Mariposilla was growing up in idleness, caring not for the teachings of the good Sisters at the Convent, hating persistently the drawn work, trying only to be like the Americans in disobedience and manners, forgetting each day how once it was glorious to have been born a Del Valle. The result of these confidences was a second visit from Mrs. Sanderson, this time accompanied by Sidney, who at once suggested the ranch as a home for myself and Marjorie.

Mrs. Sanderson had captivated the Doña Maria with the rest of us, and had no difficulty in persuading the unfortunate woman to receive us into her household. She dilated with her usual flow upon the mutual advantages of the arrangement, until I was charmed with her disinterested kindness. Not even now do I charge the woman with a premeditated plot. If one existed then, it existed for Sidney alone—the shadow of a foul possibility. Neither do I believe that Mrs. Sanderson cared to befriend either the Doña Maria Del Valle or myself.

Our residence at the ranch might prove another opportunity for enjoyment during the winter, an added zest to the California sojourn. Picturesque situations were the chief articles in the woman's creed; to entertain Sidney, her religion.

She was so supremely worldly, so accustomed to her own selfishness, that the possibility of harm, developed by the franchise of pleasure, was not considered in her schemes for entertainment. She thought it natural and amusing "that Sid should flirt with the pretty Mariposilla," and soon played herself, with the emotions of the unsuspicious child, as a cat would have played with the life of a mouse.

In a word, when Marjorie and I had once been established at the ranch of the Doña Maria Del Valle, there would be constant opportunities for pleasure, mingled with novelty. If the hotel grew intolerable, with an influx of stupid, dissatisfied tourists, the ranch might prove a haven in which one could safely linger, sheltered from the interrogations of the irrepressible "tenderfoot." Upon the shaded veranda of the old adobe, fancy work could be pleasantly pursued, or one could simply idle the time, which in Southern California seems without limit, surrounded by congenial society and picturesque associations.

Thus it came about that, believing in the generous sympathy of my new friend, I went with my child to live in the old Spanish home of the Doña Maria Del Valle.

Pervading my satisfaction was a sincere admiration for the woman who could arrange so readily tiresome details, sequestering us, almost immediately upon our arrival in a strange country, in one of the fairest spots of the rare San Gabriel Valley.

# IV

The San Gabriel Valley, in December, is pleasant to look upon. Not as winsome as in February, when the Carnival of the year is born, but serenely beautiful. Cleansing rains have polished every ridge of the Sierra Madre, until purple cañons shine out like treasures of amethyst, while clearly defined spurs, shot with softest green, reflect the promises of the Spring.

"Old Baldy," the hoary sire of the range, gleams like a high priest. To the south, shaggy "Gray Back," and still beyond, San Jacinto, a lone fortress of alabaster on a turquoise sea, emphasize again the boundaries of the horizon. The misty veil of the long summer has lifted, disclosing an unbroken line of ravishing landscape. Every leaf and bud in the valley breathes with fresh lungs. The meadow lark, tilting upon the topmost tip of the highest pine, sings to the sky a jubilate in three pure syllables. Birds are wooing sweethearts fearlessly, for now time must not be lost, and home sites must be secured in the lacy pepper trees, before the poppies cover the foothills, or baby-blue-eyes and cream-cups fringe the roadsides.

Everything is noisy with awakening life. The rich earth teems with ambitions. Volunteer seeds are springing enthusiastically to the surface. Timid wild flowers are peeping forth each day to test the possibilities of an early season, heralded even now by the irrepressible Al Filerea, which runs riot in all directions, unconscious of its doom when the plowman invades the land.

Then it is that the oranges begin to glow like gold among green shadows, and naked deciduous trees to flush with the faintest pink of returning life. So intoxicating is the air that the saddest invalid beams with renewed hope, almost forgetting his burden beneath the delicious blue of the peaceful sky.

At the foot of the Sierra Madre lies Pasadena—"Crown of the Valley"—so named from its imperial situation. An established and aristocratic nucleus for its surrounding towns, few places are so rich in conditions to palliate or allay the sorrows and disappointments of the usual life.

South of this beautiful town, where wealth and culture have displaced the primitive ranch, ordaining in its place extensive villa sites, ornate with lawns of blue grass, bordered by rose gardens and ornamental shrubbery, stretch the fertile acres of San Gabriel. Still utilitarian in their scheme, these acres comprise ranches that radiate for miles in all directions from the Old Mission, like spokes from an antiquated hub. Close to the old church are the houses and stores of the once thriving village, now, alas! dusky with memories of the Señora, the captivating Señorita, the valiant Don, and the watchful Padre.

Defenseless in its degeneracy, the place now boasts a motley population of low-bred Mexicans and narrow-eyed Celestials. Still, when the old Spanish bells call to the early Sabbath mass, if one is observing, he may find among the weather-beaten countenances of the Mexicans, often marked with the high cheek bone of the Indian, true descendants of the early aristocracy, holding aloof from the horde, absorbed in prayers, that alone are the same since the ranches were ruthlessly divided and railroads allowed to invade.

Yet the Spanish homes that remain in the valley are mere echoes of former times, but tiny specks upon the map of the real estate dealer, which have miraculously escaped the clutches of strangers. Although humble, a few of these homes are strikingly picturesque.

On a retired road, sheltered on either side by mammoth pepper trees, east of the Mission by several miles, lived the Doña Maria Del Valle. Her little ranch was all that she had saved from her husband's estate, and she ever scorned its importance when she told indignantly how her husband's father had once held a splendid principality comprising four thousand acres.

"Now, alas! we own nothing," she said, resting, a moment, her dark hands from their incessant labor at the exquisite drawn work. "My child will be always poor, she will grow like the Americans, caring not for the past. It is cruel indeed that she saw not her noble father Don Arturo. Had he but lived, with his learning and accomplishments, his child would rejoice that she was born a Del Valle! Now she listens not patiently to the tale of former days, for in the Convent she has met American girls, and thinks only to imitate them, hoping to gain for herself a strange husband who loves not her people. Our dear Arturo she scorns! driving him far away by her wicked disobedience; for when she laughed at his love he could no longer endure to behold her."

Unhappy indeed was the Doña Maria when indulging in such confidences; but not often did she speak of her troubles, for so poor had the family become, that, to support her aged mother and the pretty Mariposilla, she was compelled to work constantly at the drawn work, learned in her youth as a pastime, now, alas! one of her chief sources of revenue.

It was owing to her reduced circumstances that the proud Doña Maria had received under her roof Marjorie and myself, for she loved not the Americans; but, as she told me artlessly one day, "Only the Americans now have gold.

"Once it was not so. We, too, had gold in abundance, but we loved not our gold as the Americans love theirs, to keep in the bank. We loved gold because it gave us joy to buy land, and cattle, and jewels, and lace."

Yes, it was simply for our gold that Marjorie and I had been received under the roof of the Del Valles. Still, when once the arrangement had been entered upon, the Doña Maria was all that we could desire as a hostess.

Marjorie stole each hour into the hearts of the old grandmother and the proud disappointed daughter, aging so fast under stress of multiplied troubles, that she needed just such an appealing interest as my delicate child to call into action the unselfish side of her noble nature. Before we had lived long at the ranch our lives were running together as smoothly as if we all rejoiced in the same blood.

The house of the Doña Maria Del Valle was not the original ranch house, but a smaller adobe, built after many of the broad acres had been bartered away by the taking of imperfect securities, the worthlessness of which the happy-go-lucky owners had failed to comprehend until too late to obviate the consequences.

"We understood not the laws and the papers of the Americans," the Doña Maria explained, as we sat, one sunshiny morning, upon the sheltered veranda. "One day we owned all the land in the valley for many miles, the next day we owned not so much, and at last only the little that is left."

To me, the fifteen remaining acres appeared most desirable, for I was not then versed in the matter of fruit culture. I did not understand that orange trees differ one from another in point of perfection as widely as do people.

It was some time before I learned that in the early settlement of the valley disastrous experiments had been made. Many of the first trees planted had yielded an inferior variety of fruit, not lucrative in a market each year growing more critical, as the country became settled by determined agriculturists, who possessed, not only cash capital, but brains stimulated by college education and practical experience. Such men soon discovered that it was unprofitable to irrigate or nurture for long a tree that was not all that a tree of its kind should be.

Consequently there had been frequent upheavals of earth; many old orchards were regarded by the experienced as worthless, the owners preferring to replant with the best varieties of budded trees, even though a considerable time must elapse before a revenue would result. Unfortunately, the orange ranch of the Doña Maria Del Valle was a poor one. It was planted with a flavorless variety of seedling, which yielded an income quite insufficient for the demands of the family. From an æsthetic point of view the grove appeared the Garden of the Hesperides. The staunch, far-reaching limbs of the old trees drooped opulently beneath the golden balls that invited the "Forty Thieves," who, happening to be "tenderfeet," ate with wry faces and discourteous exclamations the fruit that a native would have scorned to touch. For in California oranges are not ripe in December. Not until the late spring, when the sun has used persistently his winsome inducements, does the fruit consent to assume its luscious perfection.

Turning from the highway, the ranch of the Doña Maria Del Valle was entered from between two mammoth century plants, whose giant spears made formidable the approach to the long avenue leading to the house. The drive was shaded by gnarled old pepper trees, uniting from each side their fantastic branches to form an elfin tunnel of lacy shade. On the ground, thickly scattered, lay dartlike leaves, and scarlet berries shading from rich to pale, until a long oriental rug seemed spread for the court of an expected princess.

At the end of the Avenue stood the low adobe, covered with ivy and the famous Gold of Ophir rose, which at Easter illuminated the veranda and roof with the lights and shadows of forty thousand blooms. Not far from the house two giant palms—honored patriarchs of the valley—reared their trembling feathers to the sky. Like grim sentinels, true to a trust, they guarded in dumb eloquence the story of the past.

Before reaching the house the drive divided, encircling within the arms of its curve a soft oval cushion of Bermuda grass that in December is brown and unpromising, but in the spring grows green remaining so through the long summer, making no imperative demand for water, and being at all seasons as soft to the feet as the most luxurious rug. It is the grass created for the invalid. He alone appreciates the thick, delicious mat, which hoards for his bloodless feet thousands of warm sunbeams that cheat his physician into the belief that he is eminent, when he discovers his patient escaping his professional clutches.

Added to the tropical effect of full-grown palms and riotous shrubbery, the guardian Sierra Madre was ever flashing rich shadows and tender patches of light, that, in the clear, prismatic air, reflected countless expressions into the hearts of the flowers and onto the surface of the leaves.

Such was the home of the Doña Maria Del Valle. Here Mariposilla had been born, sixteen years before, five months after the death of her father, Don Arturo.

# V

E ach year, when the Gold of Ophir illuminates the valley with its passionate bloom, I think of Mariposilla. Under the spell of the transient radiance of the rose, her beauty comes to me like a lovely dream. The flashing lights and subtle shades of the marvelous flower seem to communicate a wild sensation of the child's presence; for ever since I first beheld her close to the rose, there has been in my mind a fancy that between these two children of the valley there existed a bond, an almost supernatural kinship, that betrayed itself with each quiver of the atmosphere.

So impressed I became with the idea, that I unconsciously sought for Mariposilla's mood in the changing color of the rose. During the eventful weeks of which I shall write, when the rose and the girl began and finished their one exciting drama, bursting together into fullest perfection, I found myself associating them constantly in my thoughts. So essential each appeared to the other, that when Mariposilla stood beneath the Gold of Ophir she seemed to absorb its every tint, while at the same time its golden sprays glowed with the effulgence of her glorious proximity. Their harmony appeared perfect, their united beauty the personification of carnal and ethereal blending. When the sun shone early, with no rebuff from the occasional fog, thousands of buds and blossoms bloomed upon the somber adobe, and even while one looked, indescribable tones of gold, and pink, and yellow appeared to creep from the passionate hearts of the buds onto the glorified edges of the full-blown flowers. Then, too, Mariposilla dazzled. Her very being flashed with a phosphorescence akin to nothing human, but so like the luster of the rose that each must have been created that the other might bloom. Both seemed children of the sun, entrusted with opalescent secrets that nothing but his rays could reveal; for, if the day grew chill, both Mariposilla and the Gold of Ophir paled. The fire left the edges of the rose petals, and the blood retreated from the surface of the girl's creamy flesh. Her great luminous eyes grew dull, as she sought listlessly her neglected lace frame, drawing silently the threads of the linen, ignoring the whining questions of her old grandmother, completely lost in the indifference of her mood.

Or perhaps, disregarding the commands of her mother, she tossed aside the lace frame and crept into a silent corner of the room to play upon her guitar wild, turbulent music, until the Doña Maria, angry and impatient, commanded her to finish at once the altar cloth ordered months before by the lady from Pasadena. At the same time she bade her mind with care to cross herself at the little Jesus stitch, else a curse would come upon them all.

Even yet I dread to think of this strange child out of the sunshine. I would always have kept her under the influence of soothing warmth. Mariposilla—little butterfly—how well she idealized her name. Born of the sun and for the sun, no real butterfly ever rivaled her. Why could I not protect her passionate, capricious young heart, as the flowers enfold at night the dazzling, thoughtless beauties of a summer's day? Alas! destiny seemed kinder to the insect than to the child.

Viewing in retrospect the girl's rapid and eventful development, I now remember vividly each incident in her little history. When she came into my life like a picturesque plaything, I failed to realize that she was other than a beautiful child. I was then totally ignorant from experience of the premature blooming of Spanish girls. From history I knew that they developed young; but history is easily forgotten. It was natural to expect Mariposilla to pursue the same pace that once upon a time I had taken myself. We are all miserable egotists, without realizing the weakness; and I fell at once into the fallacy of believing that all girls develop in the same way. Mariposilla was only sixteen, and at sixteen most girls are children. I recalled my own blushes, as I remembered drawing-room miseries to which I was at that age subjected. When my grown brothers insisted upon presenting me to college chums, I flew at my earliest opportunity from the ordeal, cheered by the thought of a toboggan slide with my nice boy beau. Yes, I had a boy beau, who was truly delightful. It was only when he went away to college that I ceased to care for him, and bestowed my smiles upon a new flame across the way, who was yet a boy. At sixteen I regarded men as formidable creatures, to be encountered when school days were over, and childhood had come to an end. When I heard later that my gay Freshman smoked! and was engaged to a young woman of his college town, six years his senior, I wondered how I had ever consented to sit upon a sled with such a monster. At sixteen my ideas of love were as vague as they were wholesome. In my young healthiness I doubted seriously if any girl ever died for love outside of a book. Thus recalling my own girlhood, I at first felt no misgivings in exposing Mariposilla to the apparently innocent attentions of Mr. Sidney Sanderson, especially as his mother and myself were always about. It seemed only sensible to believe that the Spanish child would receive real benefit from her new associations. I did not realize the narrow boundaries of her young life, nor did I then understand how she adored Americans, whom she regarded as models of refinement and wisdom. When the Doña Maria told me of her grandnephew's love for her daughter I felt it an outrage that so young a girl should have been spoken to about marriage.

I was secretly glad that Mariposilla had repulsed her second cousin, and I could not cease to wonder why the Doña Maria, so sensible in most respects, should desire her only child to accept at sixteen the only man she had ever known. It delighted me to believe that Mariposilla found full enjoyment in the society of Marjorie. They were great friends, and at times Marjorie seemed almost as mature as the older girl. Each day they played with the hounds upon the Bermuda grass, as happy and free from responsibility as the dogs. Thus time slipped away. Peace and contentment filled our lives, while my child and her Spanish playmate rivaled each day in healthy beauty the roses, now responding to the first welcome rains.

# VI

As Christmas approached, I found myself anticipating the festal time with a restored interest as keen as the feigned enthusiasms of the previous holiday season had been unbearable. But three weeks remained of the old year, and already the new one seemed full of promises.

As I watched Marjorie and Mariposilla romp like kittens upon the Bermuda grass, I wondered if my heart could ever ache again with the old, tiresome pain. The morning was glorious, and I felt myself buoyed above my most ardent hopes. Our new life was an elixir, that drove away sad thoughts, while it invited pleasant memories. Nature had aroused once more my sluggish sympathies, until I complied eagerly with all of her coaxing demands. When her trees swayed, their quiet motion lulled me. If her birds talked, I understood their pleasant assurances. With the sun rose my heart. When it sank slowly to rest, I waited for its good-night promise upon the mountains, and when they flushed rosiest, I, too, glowed with a rapturous trust.

With Marjorie asleep in my arms, I heard my father calling dear names to his own little girl. I felt my mother braid my hair, and saw her smile at my fresh blue ribbons. Two handsome brothers teased me about the new lover, who had driven away the other beaux. And then I felt again upon my lips this lover's first true kiss. When my child laughed in her sleep I laid her gently down, and lived once more the short, sweet romance of my life.

Each day I was learning to go alone, gradually attaining the composure of one who has survived a shock, realizing at last the odds of destiny, and the necessity of making much of comfortable opportunities.

I am describing my feelings, not that I wish to write about myself, but in order that I may be pardoned if later some may blame me for lack of perception. If I was beguiled into unsuspiciousness by the peace of my new life, I should be forgiven, for at that time God's whole creation seemed as good as in the beginning.

Christmas was coming, I have said, and Marjorie was wild with expectation. I could hear her merry treble entreating Mariposilla to tell how Santa Claus could ever come to California, where there was no snow, except upon the tops of the mountains.

When the Spanish girl failed to explain, the child grew flushed

MARY STEWART DAGGETT

and excited. Marjorie's vivid imagination was tempered by a rational appreciation of consistency, and she declared indignantly that Santa Claus always traveled in a sleigh. Without snow the reindeer would have a difficult time, and she was pathetically certain that her stocking would be quite empty upon Christmas morning. The little girl was a stubborn logician. The form of her infantile dictum was often mixed, but her mother generally perceived her difficulties, and drew from sadly-muddled premises conclusions that were entirely satisfactory to both. In the existing case she had foreseen the burst of skepticism that was now distressing the child, and was well prepared to confute her troublesome doubts. "Listen," she said, "and I will explain.

"Mariposilla ought to know that when Santa Claus comes to Southern California he always lives upon the top of 'Old Baldy.' The beautiful valley is too warm for him. So each year he builds a snow house upon the mountain, and, with his pipe and reindeer for company, he works merrily at the toys which he so skillfully fashions for the children of the far West. When his loving labor is completed, he packs the wonderful presents into a huge sleigh, and at twelve o'clock of the night before Christmas, he feeds his reindeer, and hitches them to the great sledge. When the children of the peaceful valleys are fast asleep, the dear old Saint drives gaily down the steep, white side of the great mountain. At its foot he blows a long, shrill whistle, and from the many cañons of the range come the fairies. The happy little people dearly love to be useful. They have the greatest affection for Santa Claus, and they tell him truthfully about all of his boys and girls; reporting both good and naughty ones. But most tenderly do the fairies tell of the little sick children who have come from faraway homes in the East to seek for health in the land of sunshine. When the kind Saint is sure that no child has been forgotten, he commands the fairies to finish his loving work. He can go no farther with the reindeer, and so he intrusts his beautiful gifts to the willing little helpers, who have swarmed at his call. And now, at the bidding of the Fairy Queen, thousands of lily chariots, drawn by dashing teams of bumblebees, form in long lines upon the foothills. The white chariots, with their yellow daisy wheels, are a wonderful sight in the early daylight.

"Each one has a fairy driver, dressed in a Christmas suit, made from the petals of a Maréchal Neil rose. When the chariots are at last loaded to their fullest capacity with the precious toys, old Santa Claus gives the signal to start. Then the happy drivers spring upon their high, yellow seats in the center of the chariots. Gripping firmly a long lash of blue grass, each little fellow waves farewell to dear Santa Claus, who has already started up the mountain, satisfied and happy that his holiday work is done. Not until another Christmas will the valleys feel the loving presence of the kind old Saint, for when the sun and the birds have awakened his children he will be far away. But his beautiful gifts will be hanging upon the great, white rose-trees—the Christmas trees of our summer land."

When I had finished Marjorie clapped her hands and exclaimed with delight, but Mariposilla said nothing. She was silently eloquent for several moments, until, suddenly remembering that she ought to acknowledge genius, she kissed me gently upon the cheek, much as she would have kissed the wooden image of the Virgin that stood in the Doña Maria's bedroom. Looking down into my face with her great, beautiful eyes, she said, almost reverently: "The Señora knows much; she is a great and wise Americana; I love her with great love."

Mariposilla had never before addressed me in the quaint, affectionate style of her anglicized tongue, and as I caught her in my arms, laughing at the sweet, sober compliment, I told her how I would always treasure it for her sake—the most delightful praise I had ever received.

I remember it was about this time that I first became aware of the girl's rare beauty. Suddenly she seemed to have commenced to mature, and her radiance startled me. I wondered then if such ravishing charms were to be desired, for it seemed hardly possible that she would be contented with her available destiny.

I had already seen that her thoughts were not with her countryman and kinsman, Arturo, but remote, engaged with intangible dreams of she knew not what. I could not refuse to see, at times, in her restless, unsatisfied expression, that she had outgrown the customs and associations of her race. I saw that she was consumed with admiration for Americans, attempting their fashions and manners with a determination almost pathetic.

When the Sandersons came to the ranch, and we sat upon the veranda chatting in the effervescent style of our Republic, Mariposilla listened like a charmed bird, especially if Mrs. Sanderson chanced to relate a story replete with inimitable shades and mannerisms. I am certain that the lady herself realized and exerted unduly her magnetism upon the unsophisticated girl. I often noticed her regarding with complacent amusement the worshipful expression upon Mariposilla's face. Sometimes she would abruptly summon her to her side, while she touched the dark head with her beautiful jeweled hand. Perhaps she called her a pretty name; or possibly joked her about her faith in the good stories of the great Americanos, until the child's cheeks grew opalescent with happy embarrassment. Then, before the lovely tints had paled, she would send her away for a glass of water from the deep red olla, or for a rose from a bush indicated by her fancy.

I remember that upon this particular morning I was troubling indirectly about Mariposilla, thinking that perhaps her daily association with Sidney might not be for the best. I had not then dreamed of inhuman exertions on the part of the Sandersons to entrap the child. I simply wondered if we were wise to expose the beautiful, immature girl to the constant, flattering attentions of an impossible young man.

I remember that I decided to tell her, at my earliest opportunity, that Sidney was destined to marry a New York heiress. However, as soon as the thought had taken shape in my mind, I felt indignant for imagining possibilities disagreeable enough to disturb the peace of our pleasant social conditions. I said to myself that Mariposilla was still a child, often the satisfied playmate of Marjorie. It would be easy, I was sure, to observe the slightest vibration in the direction of a love affair.

The Doña Maria had assured me that her child was hard of heart, ever scorning the devotion of lovers. Altogether I felt a ridiculous prude when the gay trap of the Sandersons suddenly dashed into the avenue.

Sidney was driving the spirited team, with his mother behind him, luxuriously wrapped for the December morning.

At the first sound of the horses' hoofs upon the driveway, Mariposilla vanished. I could see at a glance, upon her return, that she had been before the little mirror in her bedroom, for the betumbled appearance occasioned by her romp with Marjorie had disappeared; likewise she had embellished her scarlet frock with a little black velvet girdle that emphasized the costume with an irresistible touch of Spain.

I perceived that Sidney was unmistakably pleased with the child's appearance; but I could not consistently blame him for our common crime, for never before had I been so impressed with the superb type of Mariposilla's beauty.

Mrs. Sanderson was most winning. She had come, she said, in search of good company for a drive. She was going to Pasadena for two yards of yellow ribbon. Was it not absolutely delightful to drive eight miles for a couple of yards of ribbon? Such irresponsible pleasure made one scorn philanthropy. Why should one desire to reconcile happy Hottentots to Parisian costume? Why be perpetually annoyed with grave and difficult questions, when all could be easily dismissed in a drive after ribbon? She lamented that she had not come to San Gabriel years ago, before there was so little to prolong. She was sure native Californians were born without nerves. It rested her more than a whole year at a sanitarium to look at Mariposilla. What a perfect beauty she was, this minute, in her red frock. She must gain at once the Doña Maria's consent and come for a drive. All must make haste, for it was criminal to lose one moment of the morning.

Mariposilla, as usual, had stood unconsciously enthralled by Mrs. Sanderson's wonderful personality. The child had not understood the lady's ironic sallies, but the invitation to drive had been plain.

Instantly the absent, incomprehensible look fled from her eyes; they seemed suddenly bathed in lambent joy, while an emotional radiance enveloped her form. Resembling the beautiful little creature after which she had been named, she appeared to dart through the sunshine, then to vanish in the doorway of the somber adobe, like a lost meteor. Her marvelous, unstudied motions seemed the reflection of fickle twilight.

"Will she come back? or has she flown forever into an old legend of Spain?" Mrs. Sanderson demanded, tragically. "She will return as demure as a novitiate," I replied.

A few moments later the truth of the statement was verified. The girl's first intense emotions had been forcibly quieted by her desire to be thought conventional. When she reappeared, prepared for the drive, she walked slowly, almost stiffly—"like a lady," the Sisters at the Convent would have said.

She had donned a black jacket, that was fortunately too small and obliged to flare, exposing the little velvet girdle and a dash of scarlet that emulated coquettishly the breast of a robin. Her hair was carefully twisted into a girlish coil, while upon her head she wore a large, picturesque black hat.

During the drive to Pasadena she was ecstatically solemn, and it was only when she turned her profile to reply almost in monosyllables to the ingenious questions of Sidney that I discovered how happy she was. Her cheeks had again assumed wonderful tints, occasioned by a renewed realization of her exalted privileges, and I could see that she was flattered beyond her most daring expectation. Sidney, usually so reticent, had suddenly maddened into an animated inquisitor. I observed that he never allowed his eyes to leave the girl's face, when she replied modestly to his volley of direct questions.

Necessarily, these recollections have now come back to me slightly embellished by the events which quickly followed this initial drive. It must have been a comprehension of the common failure to note the signs of a disaster in time to obviate it, which led the ecclesiastical composers to insert in the general confession of the Prayer Book the clause in which the sinner bewails not only his actually committed sins, but his passive criminalities, born of neglect.

My conscience will ever ache with the knowledge of "things left undone" for Mariposilla. I know now that I should have explained more decidedly to the child the impassable width of the social gulf, even at the risk of her loving me less. I should have protected her against herself, by showing her the truth without palliation. I should have told her how fraudulent and glittering are the attentions of fashionable men, and warned her against the cruel disappointments of society.

Doubtless the child would have disregarded my wisdom, for wilful, rapturous youth is slow to accept experience secondhand. At the time, it appeared only right and natural that Mariposilla should take part in our daily pleasures, while, in justice to myself, it did not occur to me to doubt the good intentions of the Sandersons, until too late to overcome the complications which arose by degrees from our general intimacy.

# VII

I t was impossible for me to resist my impulses as we dashed through the sunshine. To be absolved from every responsibility as I breathed with joy the vigorous, sedative air—a mingled freshness of May and October—had intoxicated my nerves. Unconsciously I allowed sentiments to escape, which I usually restrained when in the society of the brilliant cynic by my side.

It seemed impossible that the most hardened wretch could be capable of criminality upon such a divine morning; and I enthusiastically aired my moral philosophy, much to the amusement of Mrs. Sanderson, who jestingly replied, as we turned from a long avenue into the principal business street of Pasadena—"As usual, my dear, you have caught entirely the local spirit of your environments. I am told that the millennium has already begun in Pasadena, and that even now there are more sanctified cranks to the acre than in any town in America."

As the lady spoke, a Salvation Army girl approached with the *War Cry*. The fresh young face peering from beneath the ugly bonnet had a demure fascination, and rebellious to the scornful expression of my companion, I dropped the requested nickel into the extended hand of the pretty fanatic. As the young woman retired to the sidewalk, Mrs. Sanderson laughed a derisive little laugh.

"I am sure you will be doing something wild if you stay in this country long," she said. "If it were not for Marjorie I should feel alarmed. The noticeable attentions of the sallow, sanctimonious priest at the hotel may yet prove dangerous. I shall feel it my duty to keep an eye upon you both."

"Pray do," I replied coldly, as we left the trap and entered a dry-goods store, gay with Christmas decorations, and crowded with shoppers.

Wending our way to the ribbon counter we found it thronged by pretty girls, chattering merrily as they selected various shades from a gay labyrinth of color, that announced a sale of remnants.

It was evident that but one damsel of the group had troubled herself to remember that the month was December, for she alone did credit to her conventional convictions. She resembled, at first glance, a properly rolled umbrella. Her tailor-made gown was severe in the extreme, and her hat and carriage were harmoniously stiff. Her companions wore cheerful, girlish costumes, ranging in variety from a white flannel tennis

MARY STEWART DAGGETT

frock, supplemented by fur cape and straw sailor hat, to the very correct street suit of the severe young woman. Bright eyes and glowing cheeks showed plainly that if cotillions were a frequent occurrence in Pasadena, as the conversation of the lassies indicated, their disastrous ravages were providentially repaired by horseback riding and tennis the year round.

We had not expected to meet friends among the merry bevy, but as the young woman of the "tailor-made" turned to leave the store, Mrs. Sanderson recognized her. She was Miss Walton, the daughter of an old friend, a wealthy New Yorker, who now lived most of his time in Pasadena.

The acknowledgement was instantaneous, and before the ladies had exchanged a dozen sentences they were joined by a younger sister who was quite a beauty.

"This encounter is delightful," said the younger girl, extending cordially a pretty bare hand slightly browned by the sun. "I am so glad you have come, for now we can have Mr. Sanderson for our cotillion. We were quite desperate for another man, as one of our dearest one-lungers has been forbidden to dance. The pretty, tall girl buying the pink ribbon is the unfortunate bereft of her partner. She will be delighted with her luck, when I tell her she is to dance with a man who will not be a responsibility."

"For shame, Ethel!" interrupted the tailor-made Miss Walton; "what will the ladies think?"

"The simple truth," replied the irrepressible Ethel. "The ladies have doubtless learned of the one drawback to our glorious climate—its dearth of able-bodied dancing men. Do you wonder, Mrs. Sanderson," the girl continued appealingly, "that we jump at the chance to dance once in a while with a man who is not delicate, who has never had a hemorrhage or organic heart trouble? Of course," she rattled on, "we have a few sound men, but this year has been an off year for the unengaged. The two dear fellows who made love collectively have gone East, so you see a new man is like balm in Gilead."

"Sidney must certainly attend the cotillion," his mother said, much amused.

"Of course he must," the girl replied, gaily. "He will be the belle of the ball. When I tell the girls confidentially that he won't have to be saved a particle, won't they dote on him? You see it is simply crushing to have the responsibility of a one-lunger for a whole evening. Delicate men are always idiotic about getting in a draught, and as stubborn as mules about not putting on overcoats when healthy people are freezing. It certainly is not pleasant to stop a man in the middle of a waltz when you see his wind giving out, or to be blamed the next day when he is absolutely ill. Of course you have to be sympathetic, send him dainties, and take him to drive as soon as he is out again, but the responsibility after a time becomes too serious to be interesting."

"Ethel!" said her sister, "what do you mean? She is really not as heartless as she appears," Miss Walton continued, turning to Mrs. Sanderson. "I trust you will make due allowance for a young lady who persists in coming to town in a tennis costume; but as my father has always allowed her to act like a barbarian, mamma and I can do nothing."

"She seems delightfully hopeless," Mrs. Sanderson replied. "We must have the pretty barbarian at San Gabriel as soon as possible. Sid would find your case most interesting, Miss Ethel, but perhaps you are not aware of his missionary tendencies?"

Ethel laughed, but Miss Walton took no pains to conceal her annoyance, although she politely seconded her sister's invitation to lunch that same day at Crown Hill.

"You shall not escape us," Ethel said, gaily, as we hesitated on account of our number, explaining that five hungry people were too many to usher unexpectedly upon even the most long-suffering cook. "Not at all," the girl declared. "Wong would be in despair if no company came, as he was expecting guests who at the last moment sent word that it would be impossible for them to come."

Her father and mother, too, were away, and "but for the delightful accident of the morning my sister and I would have been all alone," she added, convincingly.

Promising to accept the invitation at the time appointed, we left the store in search of Sidney and the children.

Looking about, we perceived the team hitched across the street, while those we sought had gone into a confectory close by. I could see Marjorie dancing in front of the door with a box of candy.

The child was still too delicate for rash experiments, and I hastily rushed to her rescue. Mrs. Sanderson cynically remarked that possibly Marjorie might find it less easy to be good than her mother, adding that if the divine climatic restraints had not proved stronger than her temptation I must be merciful. I could not help feeling irritated by the sarcastic remark, and replied with spirit. Mrs. Sanderson must have seen the uncomfortable flush that I felt mounting to my cheeks, for in her inimitable way she apologized.

"Dear little saint," she said, coaxingly; "forgive me if I am less sentimental than yourself. It is, perhaps, because I have lived too long in this stupid world to believe in it very much. Alas! I am not a poet, and my blood runs cooler every day." A half tragic expression, the suggestion of regret, darkened the woman's handsome, composed face. In an instant it fled, leaving no trace of emotion.

I was much relieved to find that Mariposilla had kindly restrained Marjorie's saccharine yearnings. The child was obediently awaiting permission to eat a chocolate cream.

Mariposilla, too, had a box of candy. Sidney gallantly handed about another, which I saw was intended to insure the Spanish girl's individual claim to the little gift he had just made her.

As we left the shop, Mrs. Sanderson's eye caught sight of a window just beyond, in which was displayed a choice collection of Indian baskets. The craze had seized the lady the year before, returning with renewed vigor, she laughingly owned, when Sidney attempted to restrain her covetous longings. Her son declared that it would even now be impossible to take home all the trash she had accumulated.

"Never mind," she insisted, "we shall look at the collection. I can see at a glance that it is a fine one, and it is not yet time to go to the Waltons'."

The collection in question, we learned, was a private one offered for sale by a boom victim, whose inflated ideas of Pasadena real estate had at one time stimulated his artistic desires to ruinous extravagance. At that time he had ransacked the country for miles around for rare baskets, regardless of price, which now he was obliged to sell.

I learned later that Mrs. Sanderson was ever upon the look-out for forced sales. Keenly alive to chances for procuring things at half price, she was always alert for the critical moment.

Her enthusiasms over the existing opportunities were those of a connoisseur loaded with the offered commodity, yet unable to endure the thought of a Philistine invasion.

She said it was wrong for her to consider the purchase of another Indian basket, but if the beautiful cora with the feathers was not so extravagant in price she might possibly add it to her collection.

The clerk in attendance now signaled the owner of the baskets from the rear of the store. The gentleman came at once, and tried in vain to convince Mrs. Sanderson that the cora with the feathers was so unusually rare that it was worth much more than the price demanded. He said pathetically that his collection was very dear to him, he loved each basket with a different degree of affection, for he had discovered them all. Each had a little history.

Dearest of all was the beautiful cora which the lady admired, and nothing but absolute necessity compelled him to part with it.

Mrs. Sanderson replied that she understood perfectly his feelings. She, too, had always been a great collector. She had even at this late day discovered baskets, and knew now of a Mexican settlement where valuable things were still in hiding. She thought she would soon go upon a tour of discovery, and perhaps she might find a cora with feathers. She was sorry not to assist the gentleman in his difficulties. She would be very fond of the feather basket, she knew, and if the price were reduced upon three larger baskets as well as upon the one she admired, she might possibly take all four. However, she had best flee from temptation. It was getting late, after twelve, and the Waltons were expecting them at one.

With her inimitable smile she bade us make haste to depart, while she sympathetically hoped, in the hearing of the obsequious clerk who opened the door, that the feather basket might soon find a purchaser who would appreciate its beauty.

As she left the store her deliberation was masterly. Before she had reached the sidewalk the clerk had motioned her back. The four baskets were hers at half their value.

# VIII

O n our way to luncheon we drove between palms and flowers, the entire length of a long, well-kept avenue. Located at its end is a group of small hills, each of which has been eagerly selected for a home site because of the incomparable advantages of the situation. Conspicuous among these knolls is Crown Hill, the home of the Waltons. Unique as an island in its individual charm, its gentle slopes are surrounded on all sides by traveled roads which define perfectly its boundaries, while they protect from intrusion the low-gabled country house which stands in the heart of six acres, cresting hospitably the hill. The landscape upon all sides is strikingly beautiful. From the south and west the pastoral harmony of the view is enhanced by a chain of wooded hills evading the advances of civilization, as they smile serenely upon extensive gardens and picturesque homes. Upon other sides glorious snow-capped mountains, glittering with Alpine splendor, intensify the rich, ever-changing tones of the long, over-lapping chain. The day was so fresh and bright that as we drove to Crown Hill a new luster seemed upon the earth. As we ascended the gentle slope, Ethel waved us a welcome from the broad veranda. When we alighted, too entranced to enter the house, the elder sister appeared.

"Is it not lovely?" Ethel cried enthusiastically, perceiving our delight at the unbroken landscape. "Don't hurry us, Margaret," the girl implored, when Miss Walton began to evince a slight nervousness at our delay in entering. "Daddy is not here to point out the unsurpassed beauties of the hill; so his own girl must see that no points are overlooked, even if luncheon does wait a minute. You see," Ethel continued as we turned slowly to enter the house, drawn by the persistent expression upon Miss Margaret's apprehensive countenance; "this place belongs to Daddy and me. Mamma and Margaret own the house in New York. Every year they go back to its dingy magnificence, and imagine themselves supremely happy. When they sit in the middle drawing-room, that looks so touchingly upon our neighbors' brick side-wall, their enjoyment is rare. The place has to be lighted all day with electric lanterns, but it matters not to these two deluded souls. They are enjoying themselves in the swell room of the house—so very oriental, don't you know?"

"Do be quiet, Ethel, and show our friends in," the elder sister implored. "Margaret is an absolute tyrant," the girl replied, leading us beyond the wide, inviting hall, into a large, sunny drawing-room that at once captivated us with its individuality.

As we entered between the portières I noticed that Mariposilla flushed with delight. The child had never before been in so lovely a room. Its warm delicacy was a strange contrast to the gaudy, half-grotesque, half-religious apartments to which she had been accustomed. Ethel, perceiving her pleasure, smiled encouragingly.

"You like my room?" she said, kindly. "It is all mine, and, to be honest, I am proud of it. You see how differently I have worked for my effects from the usual methods," she said, turning to Mrs. Sanderson, who was exclaiming over the restfulness of the furniture. "I am so glad that you are pleased," Ethel continued, "for I had much to combat before I was allowed to fire oppressive upholsterings in favor of lovely Morris cottons."

The girl had indeed caught the spirit of her semi-tropical climate; for the room was charmingly in sympathy with the world outside of the windows. The rough walls, pale yellow, in combination with the paneled ceiling and colonial casings, painted cream, had surely created a perfect background for the admirable furnishings. Never before had quaint chairs and deep couches looked so inviting as these in Morris cottons. Their creamy tone, relieved by soft browns and warm yellows, defied the sordid observer, who could never quite estimate their yard value. The broad windows were curtained in simple falls of dainty lace of open texture that excluded neither sunlight nor landscape. In the colonial fireplace burned a real fire of huge logs, that was never allowed to die out, and warmed with irresistible comfort the fresh, healthful atmosphere of the room. In unsuspected corners and in bold situations, great satsuma jars filled with ferns and tall papyrus emphasized the possibilities of a Pasadena home. Cheerful watercolors in plain white frames adorned the walls, while above the fire, an old French mirror caught from the picture-window opposite the distant shadows and sunlit spurs of the peaceful Mother Mountains. Long-stemmed roses and dear old silver candlesticks gleamed side by side upon a quaint, inviting tea-table, which, close by the glowing fire, shone like a glimpse from America's most picturesque period, adorned with the dainty relics of a colonial tea-set.

"The room is superb," Mrs. Sanderson declared, as she surveyed critically its artistic details. The rich oriental rugs and large white Angora skins thickly strewn upon the straw matting completely captivated

Mariposilla. She timidly sank her feet into a rug lying before one of the broad couches, blushing perceptibly, I thought, at the recollection of her own humble home.

The simple child was nearly frightened by the prevalent luxury, and but for the watchful attentions of Ethel, might have grown uncomfortable. With infinite tact her pretty hostess led her about, with the familiarity of a sister, often coaxing her into artless bursts of enthusiasm.

"The library is papa's success," Ethel explained as we sauntered reluctantly from the beautiful drawing room. "You see," she continued, "Papa, too, has made a California room. Excepting his books, there is hardly a vestige of civilization to be found."

It was even as the daughter had said, a room in which literature and the odor of fragrant cigars alone suggested a modern epoch. The decorations, if such they could be called, were all Indian. Rare tribe blankets covered the floor and couches, serving not only for portières, but in parts of the room for wall hangings. Against these blankets were displayed an unrivaled collection of rich old baskets. Upon one wall was stretched a gorgeous Indian genealogy, the handiwork of a gifted squaw, while the skin of a mammoth grizzly, the huge head still intact, reposed in front of the fireplace. From chimney shelf to ceiling hung weapons and finery pertaining to the aboriginal chase.

"Now," said Ethel, when Miss Margaret demanded once more our immediate attendance upon luncheon, "we will strike for high civilization—my sister's own kingdom!" Upon seating ourselves about the great round table in the perfectly appointed dining-room, I observed that Sidney had been placed between Ethel and Mariposilla, while Marjorie and I had been assigned places opposite. I could see Mariposilla's every motion without appearing to watch her, and I confess that I was at first slightly agitated, fearing the ordeal might prove embarrassing, not only for the child, but for ourselves.

I was sure that she had never before been seated at so stylish a lunch-table. In spite of its cultivated informality, there was for the unsophisticated girl an unintelligible problem close at hand in the complicated appointments of her plate.

While we spoke of the exquisite long-stemmed pink roses that filled a cut-glass punch-bowl in the center of the table, I could see Mariposilla regarding quietly the array of silver encompassing her place. If I again doubted the propriety of what we had done, it was evident that but one method of escape remained—to make plain my every motion. Even as the idea seized me I perceived that the Spanish child had hit upon the plan herself, and was nervefully determined not to disgrace her friends.

As luncheon proceeded I almost forgot my fears in admiration for the child's pluck. Her sensible, observant conduct delighted me, and I no longer doubted her fitness for any social position to which she might be raised.

Mrs. Sanderson, as usual, captivated the party with gay sallies of wit. Her pretty allusions to the faultless details of Miss Walton's table won for her at once Miss Margaret's approval.

"Your starched Celestial fills me with reverence," she declared, when the impassible Wong left the dining-room, after depositing, with majestic importance, a wonderful salad.

"He never allows the maid to bring in the salad," Ethel explained, mirthfully. "He considers a salad the culmination of his art, and generally announces for the benefit of our guests, 'Heap fine salad! Muchey good.'"

"You tempt me to set up a house in Pasadena," Mrs. Sanderson said, "if for no other reason than to eat, as often as possible before I die, a perfect salad such as this. Shall we not start an establishment at once, Sid? for the joy of a Wong who enjoys entertaining as much as does his mistress? Can you invite friends in this irresponsible way at any time?" the lady asked, earnestly.

"Oh, yes," answered Ethel, "nothing delights Wong so much as company. You know, a good Chinese servant is quite ignorant of his spinal organism. He expects to serve you well for what you pay him, exonerating you delightfully from the heavy obligations often imposed in America by ambitious females who assist at cooking for a pastime."

"Then you really don't have to hold a preliminary caucus to ascertain the state of the cook's health and temper before you can find courage to invite a few friends to dinner?" Mrs. Sanderson answered, interrogatively.

"Certainly not!" said Ethel. "A good Chinaman has the greatest reverence for caste; his respect for his mistress depends largely upon what he shrewdly determines in regard to her position in society. 'She very high-tone lady,' is his favorite expression for a thoroughly admired mistress. He considers it an honor not only to serve her to the best of his ability, but regards her friends with equal consideration."

"How delightfully comfortable it all sounds! Yet is there not a possibility of converting these same convenient heathen into a state of uselessness, rather than to Christianity?" Mrs. Sanderson pursued. "I have heard," the lady continued, "that enthusiasts are already metamorphosing some of the best cooks into poets and orators, as well as first-class laundrymen into political economists."

"Now," laughed Ethel, "you are tramping poor Margaret's toes. When we first came to California my sister approved warmly of the education of the downtrodden Celestial, but I fear that experience has withered her philanthropy. One boy that we had, after professing a most devout conversion, which necessitated his departure to school at the most inconvenient times, suddenly conceived a renewed longing for the exciting informalities of Chinese New Year.

"He told Margaret, as he bade her a polite good morning, that he 'no likey be good velly long. Have more fun be heap bad some time. Good Boss forgive sins all samey when you be heap solly after while.' Even sister was crushed by the theology. Our next boy was a genuine heathen."

"I am astonished, Ethel," said Miss Walton, "I hope you will never again repeat that blasphemous story."

"Forgive her," entreated Mrs. Sanderson, "I would not have missed it for a great deal, and although it seems unfortunate that our romantic philanthropy is often quenched by a downpour of common sense, yet it is perhaps safest for the world after all. I shall never cease to enjoy your story, Miss Ethel. When my sympathies threaten to melt my judgments I shall think of your theological heathen who rose superior to his instructors, able to grasp so cleverly the pleasant features of Christianity without its inconveniences."

When Mrs. Sanderson finished her irreligious sally, Miss Walton's pained, shocked expression was most apparent. She concentrated her attention upon her jelly, with a well-bred annoyance that was readily understood by the offender. The calculating woman, with no desire to anger the truly conscientious girl, whose sectarian delight in the teachings of her church made it impossible for her to tolerate the semblance of skepticism, gracefully shifted the conversation to the engrossing cotillion, afterward bearing down with conciliatory intent upon the Christmas bazar soon to be held by the Guild of Miss Margaret's church.

"We will all come," she said, as we left the table. "One soon loses step with events in San Gabriel, but the bazar will help us to catch up with the world," she added, mirthfully.

That Mrs. Sanderson was a scoffer of the most captivating and dangerous type can not be denied. She loved to ridicule uninteresting things and commonplace people; and doubtless this fact accounted for the dearth of friends answering to her own age. It was to unthinking youth that the flashing sarcasms and stinging flings at established usages and sacred traditions appeared the embodiment of brilliant repartee. In complete contradiction to her caustic beliefs, she seemed to the young the soul of sincerity, working ever the most unselfish conditions for their enjoyment.

Mrs. Sanderson disliked old people inhumanly, while she courted, with every possible inducement, the society of the young.

"I have a morbid horror of growing old," she would say. "Sid won't promise to poison me, so I suppose I must provide myself with a daughter-in-law. My best blood is French, and when the illusions are once dispelled each new wrinkle will torture." On the day of the luncheon, as we sauntered from the drawing-room into the library, Mrs. Sanderson declared that she had conceived an idea for old age. "Your father's study is an inspiration," she exclaimed, turning to Ethel. "As soon as I am sixty I shall take down all the mirrors in my house and prepare a similar retiring room, although more entirely barbaric. There shall be no vestige of civilization in my den, nothing to encourage reminiscences, nothing to suggest the masterful march of time. I see now that it is the certainty of one's period which crushes. Indian decorations mean absolutely nothing to the uninitiated. Wrapped in the blanket of a remote chief one could forget even his birthday. There shall be nothing in my room to remind me every hour that I am a grandmother. Nothing to say—'You bought me thirty years ago,' or, 'We are both growing threadbare together. Your hair is white and thin, while I am quite out of style.' No, my dears, if I live to be old, I shall never be tortured by relics of my own period. However," the cold, worldly woman continued, smiling irresistibly upon her young companions, who failed to comprehend her heartless theories, "I am not sixty. I have several years before I must take to a blanket, so let us return to the pretty drawing-room and Mariposilla will play one of her witching Spanish dances."

"Be spry, Sid," she commanded, when the Spanish child obediently seated herself upon a low chair preparatory to tuning the guitar, "a footstool for the little feet; they look so pretty upon a cushion."

The lady's open flattery appeared no longer to embarrass Mariposilla;

she was gradually growing accustomed to that, but when Sidney placed in front of her the footstool, a richer flush intensified her beauty.

"She must have a mantilla for her head," Mrs. Sanderson cried, as she caught from her own shoulders the rich Spanish lace scarf, which she wore in her drives as a throat protector. She threw it lightly over the girl's dark head, allowing the ends to fall about her scarlet frock. "There! is she not a divine señorita?" she exclaimed, as she viewed her blushing plaything with critical delight. "Is she not exquisite?" she continued shamelessly. "See how easily we have caught the loveliest butterfly in all Old Spain! Play! Mariposilla, play!"

When the child obediently struck the strings of the guitar, Mrs. Sanderson declared that American women knew nothing of dress. "Why do we not burn our bonnets, that our lovers may kneel to our lace mantillas?" she said to Ethel.

As Mariposilla paused in her playing, all applauded with the exception of Miss Walton. From the first, she had appeared annoyed by the dramatic conditions of the afternoon. As our hostess, she was oppressed with suppression. I could see that the literal young woman, viewing all things from a narrow and conventional standpoint, longed to escape from the theatrical atmosphere which Mrs. Sanderson had so unexpectedly created.

I myself may have doubted the propriety of Mrs. Sanderson's course, but at the time, I did not doubt the woman, and was so completely bewitched by Mariposilla's beauty, that I failed to disapprove what appeared to be only a pleasant pastime.

Never before had I seen any one so lovely as this young girl. The rich tints had kindled beneath her cheeks, while her eyes, when she lifted them, shone with lambent reflections of wonderful, half-understood joy. She appeared a vision from a lost century, playing upon the credulity of the present.

I do not wish to give the impression that Mariposilla was a marvelous musician, for such was not the case. She only played with an original abandon which made her movements and the customary little tricks of her instrument appear more masterly than in reality they were. Her playing depended entirely upon her mood, and that she was now happy, carried far away from vexation or possible disappointment, was plain; for the slender brown fingers picked the strings as never before. She seemed perfectly absorbed in her music, and only when the long lashes lifted for a moment did her wonderful eyes proclaim the truth she was attempting to hide. When the lashes again drooped, soft, telltale shadows quivered beneath the dark fringe that hid her impassioned joy. The ridges of her small ears grew pink, her lips richer. The merest reflection of dimples fled and returned to the glowing cheeks, as each new emotion revealed her happy secret.

The day, I have said, had been unusually warm. The sun had reached its meridian without faltering; only above the mountains had the fathomless blue of the sky been broken by a few thin clouds. Unexpectedly the air grew chill as the sun fled behind a bank of fog, which spread each moment with amazing density upon the valley.

With the first dimming of the day, a change appeared in Mariposilla; while Miss Walton grew at once serene. Unexpectedly and discordantly the Spanish child ended her performance. Like a frightened bird she fluttered to my side, her color gone, her courage shaken.

"We must go," I said, turning to Mrs. Sanderson. "Marjorie must not be exposed to the fog," I explained, as we bade good bye to Miss Walton and Ethel. There appeared to be a mock significance in Miss Margaret's thin voice when she invited us to repeat our visit. Ethel alone accompanied us to the door.

# IX

Never before had the unpretentious home of the Doña Maria Del Valle appeared so complete a refuge as upon our return after the eventful day in Pasadena. In the living-room our kind hostess had lighted a fire of grotesque grape roots, that writhed like a holocaust of mummies. After the gloom without, our welcome seemed perfect. The ruddy flames from the fireplace, flickering against the dusky walls, had mercifully relieved the row of saints, who in the daytime appeared to suffer persistently the throes of indigestion. Likewise, from her frame above the chimney shelf the little Spanish Virgin smiled serenely upon her holy Child. In the firelight, she seemed to forget her atrocious finery in the sweet consciousness of her maternity.

The aged grandmother dozed in her accustomed chair. At her feet the grayhounds, Pancho and Pachita, sprawled in longitudinal grace, dead dogs, to all appearances, until a trespassing footstep attested their vigilance.

A faint, delicious odor of frijoles floated from the kitchen when the Doña Maria opened the door to bid us welcome home.

Marjorie flew to the strong arms overjoyed; but Mariposilla avoided her mother as she hastily retreated to her own room, remaining apart until called to supper.

The watchful Doña Maria, observing that her child could eat nothing, artlessly inquired the cause. "Are not the frijoles inviting?" she asked, in simple distress. "I have prepared them most fresh, and the oil is from a new bottle," the good woman pursued.

"Perhaps my child is not well; if so, it is unfortunate that she should have gone from home, for the good Father and Sister Francisco came at noon. While I served them with fruit and wine the Father told much of our dear Arturo, expressing often great joy that so fine a youth grows rich, soon to return to the friends who await him with so much affection. Sister Francisco was grieved that the convent is no more dear to her child. She requested that the days be few until a visit is paid, and left with her love a little gift."

As the Doña Maria paused, she arose from the table and handed Mariposilla a small religious book.

The child had controlled herself with stoical determination throughout her mother's reproachful disclosures, but, unable to do so longer, she burst into tears and fled from the room.

The calm Doña Maria took no notice of the tempestuous departure, but the grandmother appeared distressed, muttering her disapproval in Spanish.

I confess that I felt annoyed at Mariposilla's conduct. I could see no reason for the outburst of grief and felt myself an innocent agent in unsettling her happiness and disturbing her family.

After supper, when I had undressed Marjorie, who was soon asleep, and had put on a chamber gown preparatory to writing letters, a timid tap at my door told me that Mariposilla was without. So fond had I become of the child that I instantly forgot my recent resentment. Not waiting for the penitent to come to me I met her at the door. Drawing her to the couch I urged her to tell me quietly the cause of her unhappiness.

"The señora will think me unworthy of her love," she cried, chokingly.

"No, dear," I replied, "I shall always love you. I have had many sorrows myself, and I know how hard it is to speak of them; but always when I have confided in a true friend, I have felt better and sorry that I had not sought relief sooner."

"I will tell you," she said, "and then you may despise me."

She was very beautiful as she half drooped before me, her great eyes moist, her dark hair loose about her shoulders.

"Tell me all, dear child," I urged, as she still hesitated.

"I am most wicked!" she cried desperately. "I love not my people; I am unhappy because I am not an American."

A gush of tears terminated the confession.

"Poor child!" I said, drawing her to my side; "I am glad that you have told me your trouble, for I think I can help you very soon."

She lifted her face appealingly while I spoke.

"Yes," I continued, "I am sure that I understand your unhappiness. You are not untrue to your people. You only desire to be an American because you have perceived that they are more in touch with the times than your own nation, who, from loss of fortune and other causes, are not what they once were, or what they will some day be again. Your poor little heart and mind are starving for food. You must be nourished, and then you will be happy. It is perfectly right that you should admire the superior attainments and polished manners of a race not your own. It means no disloyalty to your people, only the desire for a broader life and a higher culture.

"You may be sure, dear child, that no one is ever satisfied. The yearnings of the heart after unattainable desires is common in God's wide creation. The longings of the savage are only different in degree from yours or mine. Race puts no limits upon pure and laudable ambition.

"It is not necessary for you to be an American to be all that a lovely woman should be. The daughter of the brave, wonderful Doña Maria Del Valle can make of herself whatever she determines."

Mariposilla was still weeping gently.

"You are very beautiful, dear child," I continued. "More beautiful than any American girl I ever knew. Still there is a beauty which shines from the soul and from the mind that you must try daily to acquire. Then you will be lovely, without flaw.

"If only you will be patient and true to your best ambitions, I am sure that a great happiness will some day come into your life. Try to be contented. Be a dutiful daughter to your dear mother, who has seen so much sorrow, and has left only her precious child. Please her in all things that are possible, and if you will do this I am sure that after a time you will understand how wise and unselfish she has always been."

Instantly the girl released herself, while she faced me with a passionate despair I will never forget.

"I will do all," she cried, "but marry Arturo. If I do not that I have done nothing. The priest and my mother and the sisters at the convent will curse me if I refuse. They will call me a shame, and, although I love not Arturo, they would sell me for his gold."

"No, dear," I entreated, "no one will compel you to marry Arturo. Believe me, you shall do as you please, only you must not allow unjust suspicions to make you miserable. Think no more for the present of marriage, try only to learn things that will fit you for life and happiness; after a time, if one should come whom you love, you can then not only make him joyful with your great beauty, but he will love and respect you, because you have acquired the knowledge that makes life agreeable and comfortable long after youth and beauty have flown."

"The señora is most wise," the child assented calmly. "Perhaps she will teach me a little from her books, that I, too, may learn of the great world; for, indeed, I will be good," she cried, brightening with the determination.

"Yes, Mariposilla," I replied; "each day you shall have a lesson in English, and soon you will be able to enjoy all that I enjoy; only in return you must teach me Spanish, that I may also understand the language and literature of your famous race."

Thus the compact was sealed, and each day afterward found Mariposilla seated quietly in my room, poring over an allotted task. Her stormy passions seemed stilled. If the wind of destiny sometimes shrieked in my watchful ears, it more frequently sighed plaintively as I devised new educational schemes for my protégée.

No one was more delighted over Mariposilla's apparent reformation than the Doña Maria.

Not only did the lessons progress with astonishing regularity, but work on the altar cloth, which had been for long intervals neglected so that its various stages of completion were easily detected in the several soiled sections of the linen, was resumed with steady, plodding determination. Now but one row of the little Jesus stitch remained to be done in the beautiful cloth ordered months before by a wealthy devotee.

The Doña Maria was in ecstasies when her daughter brought the task finished, two days before Christmas; at the same time begging permission to ride to Pasadena that she might receive for her labor the great sum of thirty dollars.

That same morning, when Mariposilla was pressing carefully the handsome piece of linen, Father Ramirez had looked into the kitchen and praised her industry.

"After all, she is a dear child," the old priest said, patting the dark head. "She will yet make a true woman like her dear mother. Before long Arturo will come, and the bells of Old San Gabriel shall ring again as they rang for the Doña Maria long ago."

Mariposilla flushed not. A deadly pallor extinguished the healthy glow that the light labor had produced. Turning disrespectfully away, she darted through the open door, and was gone.

It was only after the old priest had left and the Sandersons had driven into the long green tunnel that color shone again beneath the surface of her cheeks.

# X

The Sandersons did not remain long at the ranch. After their departure Mariposilla saddled the pony, and, bidding us a gleeful adieu, cantered away with the precious altar cloth.

At parting, the Doña Maria had given her child, for a surprise, a dozen exquisite doilies of her own workmanship. They were bestowed as a reward for the girl's recent industry, and she was permitted to sell them with the altar cloth.

"Shall I not be rich?" she cried, brandishing in excitement a superb riding whip, a remnant of former glories. "When I am come again the señora will go with me to Los Angeles. There I shall buy beautiful things for you all."

An instant later she was flying down the green tunnel. As she passed between the mammoth century plants, she waved once more her whip—and was gone.

"Dear child!" I said, as we entered the house.

"Yes," said the mother, "she is good of heart. If only she would listen to the advice of Father Ramirez and marry Arturo, we might all be once more joyful."

"Yes," I answered, "I hope it may yet be as you desire; but, if you will pardon me, dear Doña Maria, for speaking plainly, let no priest or other person come between your child and yourself. Mariposilla is still so young that she is absolutely frightened at the thought of marriage. Let her develop gradually in her own way, willful though it may appear.

"I am sure that after a time, when Arturo returns, handsome and successful, she will accept his proffered love."

The Doña Maria's great, sad eyes filled with happy tears. "Blessings be on you, dear lady!" she said; "I shall ever be happy that it has been sweet to have given you our home."

Kind Doña Maria! it was exactly what she had done—she had given us her home. Generously, she had taken two strangers into her great motherly heart to dwell.

Mrs. Sanderson was to come this same afternoon, for a lesson in drawn work.

As I dropped into my accustomed nook of the veranda, the industrious Doña Maria hastened out to the kitchen to perform a remaining duty. Then, before she had made the still rich, dark hair tidy, and perhaps said a prayer to the little wooden Virgin in the corner of her bedroom, her pupil had arrived. Mrs. Sanderson was driven by a groom; her son was not with her.

Sidney had gone coursing with some people from East San Gabriel who kept hounds, she explained.

I remember that I wondered instantly if the man had followed Mariposilla.

As it was impossible to know, I could only appear interested in the progress of the drawn work. For some unknown reason the lesson soon lagged. Mrs. Sanderson grew irritable over her indifferent success, and for the first time wearied me a little.

The lady was in one of her intolerant moods. Her captious rejoinders and censorious criticisms upon the guests of the hotel annoyed me. I realized for the first time that possibly I myself might sometime become a target for my capricious friend's sarcasms.

Marjorie wanted to go for a walk, so, excusing myself, we departed.

Holding my little one's hand, I tried to forget, in her sweet, unconscious talk, the caustic brilliancy of the woman I had left. Every stray dog or resting bird that enlivened our walk delighted the child. When we came to some anthills she grew flushed and excited as she built a fence about the thriving city to protect it against the invasion of tarantulas.

Ever since Antonio, the Mexican, had unearthed a tarantula one morning in the corner of the orchard, Marjorie had regarded the ugly yet comparatively harmless creature as California's one demon. Romancing in her play, she slew the formidable monsters in single imaginary combat, enjoying among the birds and butterflies the same enviable notoriety that St. Patrick attained when the snakes fled from the Emerald Isle.

Watching my child at play, I scarcely realized that the short winter day was rapidly settling into twilight. At once hastening home, we found Mrs. Sanderson gone and the Doña Maria busy preparing supper. Half an hour later it was dark and Mariposilla had not yet come.

I could see that the Doña Maria was uneasy, for she went often to the door, once as far as the turn in the driveway. Supper was now waiting. The frijoles were in steaming readiness, and yet Mariposilla was absent.

All were growing alarmed, when the dashing of horses' hoofs told me that not one but two persons had arrived. In a moment, I had flashed the light of the room through the open door into the night.

MARY STEWART DAGGETT

I heard distinctly the sweet, low voice of Mariposilla and saw her lifted to the ground from her pony. In the uncertain light the strong arms of Sidney Sanderson appeared to poise dangerously long the girlish form that resisted not the delay of the transit.

I doubt if the Doña Maria saw what I believed that I saw, for at the time I think she had turned to speak to the anxious grandmother; then, satisfied that the child had returned, she left the room.

The barking of the vigilant dogs had drawn me instantly to the door, and I remember how positively certain I then felt that Sidney had kissed Mariposilla during her groundward journey.

At the moment I believed entirely that he had done this thing, I was filled with indignation, and ready to denounce him fearlessly, until Mariposilla, bounding to my side, radiantly innocent, from the uncertain darkness, implored me to assist in detaining for supper the kind friend who had proved himself so invaluable during the afternoon. I stood bewildered as the child proceeded to disarm my suspicions. Calling her mother from the kitchen, she begged her to press the invitation that Sidney was hesitating to accept.

That Mariposilla could be acting a part seemed impossible. Involuntarily I followed the girl from her disappearance between the century plants early in the afternoon, up to the present time, when she stood before me, dazzling and lovely, telling what to all appearance was nothing but the truth.

As we seated ourselves about the supper table, I knew that my suspicions were rapidly subsiding. Later I denounced myself humbly, for allowing my imagination the absolute freedom of the night.

Sidney had never before appeared so manly or straightforward. He seemed highly amused at Mariposilla's ecstasy over his apparently accidental appearance upon the scene of her disasters, while he ate with innocent relish the supper which the hospitable Doña Maria delighted to serve.

"I was ruined but for Mr. Sanderson," the Spanish girl explained tragically. "I could not have gone to Los Angeles with the señora, and the precious things for Christmas could not have been bought; because I had stupidly lost the altar cloth and the gift of my mother. I was returning home miserable, without the money for which I had labored; wild with anger when I remembered how I had gone almost to Pasadena before I knew that my treasures were lost. For wicked Chiquita had shied in many places, and many strangers had passed upon the road, so

I knew that to search in hope would be useless. I could only weep upon the neck of my bad Chiquita, feeling ashamed, but unable to forget my sorrow. It was then that my friend saw me, and restored again my treasures.

"Was it not kind in our dear Lady to send him so quickly; almost as soon as I had prayed through tears one little prayer?

"Oh! it was joy to see again my things in the hand of a friend, when I had believed them found by a stranger."

As the child paused, she looked confidingly at Sidney, who smiled assent to what she had been saying.

"Yes," he affirmed with unusual animation, "I was permitted to play, for the first time in my life, the exalted rôle of the good old man who comes out of the bushes just in time to save the beautiful princess from disaster."

We all laughed, but Mariposilla sank her lovely face lower, while she regarded her plate intently.

Suddenly she lifted her great earnest eyes fearlessly to my own. They were full of light and happiness. I doubted no longer that she was innocent of what I had imagined.

"I will call the señora early," Mariposilla said, when Sidney had gone and we were parting for the night. She had been dancing about the room clicking, in imitation of castanets, her cherished gold pieces.

"Is it not grand to be rich?" she cried. "How happy I am this night! I shall never be so happy again."

She looked strangely prophetic as she spoke. She had not removed her riding habit, and, while dancing, she caught up gracefully the insubordinate skirt, which trammeled her exuberance. Floating about the room, she appeared unconscious of everything but the delights of her awakened body. Her feet and arms moved in an ecstasy of unrestraint. The abandoned sway of her agile frame caught naturally each modulation of the improvised castanets.

"Come, dear Butterfly," I said, when she threw herself panting into a chair, her eyes shining with excitement. "Fly quickly to bed or the pretty wings will be weary for the hard, long to-morrow."

"Oh, the beautiful to-morrow!" she cried, rapturously. "I will call the señora early—that not one moment of the precious day may be lost."

# XI

True to the arrangement, I heard the little bare feet patter across the hall to my door with the first gleam of the bright December morning.

The Doña Maria had prepared an early breakfast, but Mariposilla could eat nothing in her excitement. The gold pieces were carefully counted into the little purse, and the deliberate Antonio was soundly scolded for his delay in bringing around the pony hitched to the old buggy, which I earnestly hoped would not fall to pieces short of the station.

As we parted from the Doña Maria, she requested me to select a ready-made frock for Mariposilla, explaining that her daughter had been invited to spend a week at the East San Gabriel Hotel with Mrs. Sanderson.

I was so astonished at the announcement that I could hardly conceal my surprise; but the Doña Maria not appearing to notice it, I replied that I would be happy to serve her; at the same time, I decided to take Marjorie and go myself to the hotel. Mrs. Sanderson had urged us to come repeatedly, and I felt that now the invitation was imperative. Mariposilla should not go to the Sandersons' alone. I had instituted myself her guardian, and I would protect her not only from her inexperience, but from unscrupulous attentions, selfishly bestowed.

I knew that Mrs. Sanderson had secured the Doña Maria's consent for her daughter's visit to the hotel during my absence the previous afternoon; and I saw at once that Mariposilla had not known of the plan before. However, her first demonstrative joy was smothered in quiet ecstasy. All the way to the city she was rapturously solemn. Only her telltale color and her eyes confessed the exciting dreams which were filling her innocent brain.

As the purchase of the dress had now become the mainspring of our expedition, we went, at the termination of our short journey, directly to a store, announcing through show windows its distinctive claim to imported novelties. Upon the threshold we were met by a smiling French saleswoman, possibly the only genuine importation in stock, but wonderfully successful in discounting the abnormal developments of Hebrew physiognomy visible in the ever watchful proprietor.

It was but the work of a moment to abandon ourselves completely to the feminine joy of our undertaking. Once within the toils of the Frenchwoman, escape appeared the height of ingratitude.

Mariposilla was soon radiant with delight as she tried on, for the first time in her uneventful life, costume after costume, commenting innocently upon the merits of one, while she deplored the deficiencies of another. After many trials, she had almost decided to take a pretty, rich blue serge, enlivened with touches of gay plaided silk, when the wily saleswoman brought out unexpectedly from a perfumed box a beautiful dress of cream cloth.

The child held her breath as she begged to try on the wonderful frock with the jaunty, sleeveless jacket, worn over a soft, creamy silk waist, the entire costume daintily brightened with bands, embroidered in gold thread. When she stood arrayed before the long mirror, regarding affectionately the stylish puff of the sleeves, and the circular, girlish effect of the throat, outlined by a band of gold, her simple vanity forgot concealment.

"Mademoiselle is most bewitching!" the Frenchwoman exclaimed. "She can not find one other costume so becoming. Her complexion looks most perfect! So harmonious! So delightful!"

In the mirror I could see reflected Mariposilla's extravagant joy. She had never in her life before been so beautifully dressed. Instinctively she snatched from her head her hat, discovering with quick perception that its somber shabbiness detracted from the general effect of the dainty costume. Standing for a moment unconscious of the audience, she threw a kiss to her own lovely image. Realizing what she had done, she flushed deeper and turned away.

"Mademoiselle is an artist! She perceives that she looks most beautiful," the Frenchwoman pursued. "She must certainly buy the costume. There is about it an air. It has just arrived, and will soon be sold. Mademoiselle must not hesitate."

For the first time the thought of the price presented a possible drawback to the inexperienced child. She turned from the mirror, touchingly in earnest in her inquiry. "How much does it cost?" she asked.

When the saleswoman named the amount the disappointed girl began heroically to remove the jacket. As she laid it aside she turned instinctively to me for sympathy.

"I cannot pay the price," she whispered. "It would take all that I have, and there would be nothing left to buy the shawl for my mother, or the slippers for my grandmother, or the doll for Marjorie."

A moment longer she hesitated, the mist of disappointment gleaming in her eyes. Then, with a quiet resolution that was wonderful, she commanded the saleswoman to remove the coveted temptation, announcing her determination to take the blue dress which she had previously fancied.

I was delighted at the character she evinced. I knew how bitterly disappointed she was, and I was proud not only of her quiet self-control, but of the loving thoughtfulness she had displayed in remembering that her little store of gold must be divided with the toiling mother, the old grandmother, and my own little child.

"Do up both costumes," I said in undertone to the saleswoman, less attentive now that she had discovered the extent of Mariposilla's capital. Impertinently folding the discarded dress, she allowed Mariposilla to struggle as best she could with her buttons.

At my announcement she flew to assist, but I commanded tartly the packing of our purchases.

After we left the store I noticed several times during the day that the child still remembered covetously the denied frock; but she behaved sensibly, and after we had bought the shawl, and the slippers, and a Chinese doll for Marjorie, and there was still money for a sailor hat and a few trifles, she appeared satisfied. She enjoyed, with childish appetite, our elaborate luncheon; while she evinced the warmest interest in my selection of toys and books for Marjorie. When she discovered that I had bought presents for her mother and the grandmother, she seemed to have dismissed entirely the disappointment of the morning.

We left the city by a late afternoon train, and already twilight had ceased to linger. As we stepped blindly into the early winter darkness at the end of our short journey, the voice of Sidney Sanderson sounded pleasant and assuring.

"You see," he explained, as he unburdened our far-reaching arms, "I fancied you would need assistance. Antonio gratefully resigned his responsibilities, and I took the liberty of coming myself with a more substantial vehicle."

The escape from the uncertainties of the old buggy, to say nothing of the eccentricities of the pony, filled me with gratitude for our deliverer. After the tiresome day, it was truly delightful to find a friend in the depths of the darkness. As yet I had not attained the independence exhibited by many unprotected women whom I met, and Sidney's unexpected courtesy so touched my heart that I meekly determined to forget forever my suspicions of the evening before.

I had never quite overcome my childish dread of the dark, and as we stepped from the train to the wayside platform I shall never forget the sickening wave of loneliness that deluged my courage. A longing for the electric lights of the city, for the first time in months, fastened upon me; while never before had a familiar voice sounded so welcome as did Sidney's, coming from the uncanny denseness of the night. It was not until we had reached the long dark tunnel of peppers that I regained the composure which I felt continually from my first day with the Doña Maria.

Through the open door streamed a bright welcome, checking effectually my transient discontent; for midway in the flood of light danced Marjorie—a sprite in white, flushed and joyous, she watched for our return.

Within, the grape roots had been piled high. The supper table shone with unusual luster. Old silver and rich red roses proclaimed the night a gala one, and the kind Doña Maria, in her best black silk, bade us the old-time welcome of Christmas Eve.

The grandmother, resplendent in great gold ear-rings, chattered garrulously in Spanish, while Mrs. Sanderson smiled indulgently and regally upon all.

The lady was in demi-evening toilet, and the delicate tone of her French-gray gown, embellished with lace and caught at the half low throat by flashing jewels, was to Mariposilla a revelation. To the simple child the handsome woman appeared a wonderful vision, from which she could not withdraw her eyes. For the first time she beheld Mrs. Sanderson in her most captivating rôle; the conventional habit of day, exchanged for one of rare artistic beauty, had given to the lady a sudden fascinating youth which was startling. In the less impertinent light of evening, the encroachments of time were effaced. The aristocratic features and dazzling teeth belied the years of the woman whose supreme object had been their preservation. The beautiful hands, ablaze with jewels, seemed to smite the humble room with light, when the lady caressed, with amused vanity, the bewildered child she had so perfectly enthralled.

"Fly, Butterfly," she coaxed, as Mariposilla lingered by her side; "Sid is starving! and so are we all. Cast aside the old, dull frock and dazzle us in the new one."

I had always noticed that Mrs. Sanderson was exuberant in the evening. To her theatrical nature there was something exhilarating in the flicker of artificial lights. When high noon told her unpleasant truths, she forgot them the same evening, amid shaded lamps and candles. An open fire could warm her usually chilly sympathies, until she sometimes forgot her selfishness in genuine kindness. At such times, occasionally, she grew honest, and often liberal.

She had declared that misfortunes and ugly surroundings would soon make her a devil. It was only when deceived by luxury and flattery that she was capable of good thoughts.

"I am naturally depraved before I have had my bath and my early coffee," she would say, jestingly, to the amazement of the literal, whom she delighted to shock. "Sid, the scamp, knows better than to cross me before luncheon. In the evening he is safe. When he sees that I am in the ecstasies of dotage, a perfect old egotist, happy with illusions, he imposes upon me shamefully."

Strange, worldly woman that she was, it was impossible to condemn her brilliancy.

She had told us that her great grandmother was a Frenchwoman of rank, and as I regarded her this Christmas Eve, I seemed to see the proud dame of the fallen monarchy living again in the imperious form of her descendant.

I had not completed my hasty toilet when Mariposilla came flying to my door, breathless. She held in her arms the dress of cream and gold.

"See," she cried; "they have made a mistake! and I must again part with the beautiful dress. Can I not wear it this once that my friends may see it?"

I had not the heart to rebuke her; she was so lovely in her ignorance. I could only smile indulgently, as I bade her enjoy the frock, which was to be her Christmas present.

"Dear, kind Señora," she exclaimed, passionately kissing my hand; "I will indeed be good! I will indeed learn fast."

"Very well," I replied, "if you are good I shall always be glad that I was able to please you. But come, dear child," I urged; "make haste, for the Doña Maria is calling. She will be deeply annoyed if we allow her supper to cool."

It was astonishing how quickly Mariposilla complied with my command. Her transformation appeared to occupy but a moment.

And never was the awakening of an actual butterfly more surprising or triumphant.

Her joy in her enhanced beauty was rapturous and innocent. When we entered the living-room she hugged herself with delightful vanity as she approached the astonished Doña Maria.

"Am I not grand? Am I not beautiful?" she demanded. "Is not my dress more rich than the dresses in the green chest of my grandmother? Be happy with me, dear mother. Kiss thy child, and give her at last the little necklace of opals. See," she continued, coaxingly, peering into a mirror, "see how sweetly the necklace will lie against my throat; just as my beautiful Aunt Lola once wore it," she entreated in Spanish.

"Hush, foolish child," the Doña Maria commanded sternly; for at the first mention of the necklace the grandmother had shown ominous signs of dissatisfaction. When Mariposilla persistently mentioned the name of the dead Lola the old woman screamed angrily, growing each moment more excited, until the patient Doña Maria coaxed her gently from the room.

"I am so sorry," cried the penitent child, when the door closed upon the now shrieking and unmanageable Spanish woman. "I am so sorry that I compelled my grandmother to make a noise. She approves not of joy; and my mother, too, is often sad when I am happy; for she then thinks only of my dead father and the evil fortunes which have befallen us."

For answer, Mrs. Sanderson drew the unhappy girl within the charmed circle of her arms. With her soft, jeweled hands she clasped about her throat a pretty string of gold beads. "Say no more about the opal necklace," she said; "the little beads will do until you are older."

When the Doña Maria returned, Mariposilla had recovered her spirits. She was talking gaily with Sidney, unconscious of everything but the delight of the moment. As her mother approached, she flew to her side, that she might admire the necklace she had just received. With pretty entreaty she begged the Doña Maria to thank once more the dear friends who had given her so much joy.

For a moment the mother seemed to forget everything but the touching happiness of her child. A tender light shone in the great, dark eyes when she thanked us in a little speech displaying the fervent characteristics of her simple nature.

The supper was now steaming upon the table. A great platter of chicken tamales had been prepared, as none but the Doña Maria knew how to prepare them. The fragrant coffee, the dainty biscuit and the rich preserves and cream, tempted us delightfully with the unconventional perfection of Spanish hospitality.

The only restraint upon our complete enjoyment was the consciousness of the protesting grandmother. Mrs. Sanderson, I perceived, was intensely annoyed.

Her hatred of the imbecile tyranny of age was plain when the Doña Maria excused herself, finding it impossible to remain longer away from her unreasonable charge, now protesting in methodical shrieks.

"Be happy, dear friends," she said. "Mind not the infirmities of my mother. I will soon soothe her—in time—to sleep; when she will forget for a season the sorrows of her life. Make free with all that is ours, and enjoy, if possible, the supper which I have prepared. My daughter will serve, and may the night be happy!"

Dear, brave Doña Maria! how could we reverence her enough? How forget in mirth the pathos of her noble unselfishness?

Long after the Sandersons had gone, long after Mariposilla had ceased to rejoice over her splendid fortunes, forgetting in the natural slumbers of youth the caressing pressure of the gold beads, or the sweet secret of the little bracelet hugging her arm, that she must not show, but could kiss in solitude, long after the gorgeous air castles, built by the ignorant, innocent young architect, had crumbled for the night, and I had ceased to listen to the faint noises from the adjoining room, did the patient Doña Maria keep her vigil.

As I dropped to sleep I heard her tender voice soothing like an infant the aged mother, who at last sank away into a long, irresistible slumber.

When the clear, yellow dawn of Christmas morn awakened the cocks of the corral, I heard the Doña Maria knocking at her daughter's door. Opening my own I inquired if her mother still slept, begging that I might relieve for a time her patient watch.

"The Señora is kind," she said, "but my mother will now sleep for many hours. The Señora need not fear; she will scream no more. She has taken the sleeping potion, and now I am free to go with my child to the early celebration."

Mariposilla was now awake. Her hair had fallen over her shoulders and the little necklace still encircled her throat. About her eyes lingered the rosy flush of her unbroken sleep. She sat up as we entered, pushing quickly beneath her nightgown sleeve a tiny rim of gold.

"Come, my child," said the Doña Maria, "make haste and prepare for the early celebration. Our sufferer sleeps at last, and we may now go together to the church and thank once more the sweet Mother for the birth of the Holy Child."

I went back to my room as Mariposilla began to dress. A few moments later I heard the outer door close gently, and knew that the Doña Maria and her child had gone.

A strange fear fastened upon me, driving me irresistibly to the adjoining door. I opened it. The darkened room was a fascinating terror. I entered, and approached the bed of the sleeping Spanish woman. Her stillness was terrible. The old horror seized me. I felt once more the power of my old enemy. Death seemed to be facing me again. The same cruel, dreadful certainty that I knew so well! I staggered forward to flee. I must have fainted, for when I revived I was lying upon the floor in front of the little wooden Virgin. The blessed sunlight was peeping from the sides of the window curtains, while above the head of the image there hung a golden beam.

I arose and stood calmly by the bed of the Spanish woman.

The linen was spotless; the pillow cases and night-dress of the sleeper elaborate with the drawn needlework of the Doña Maria. The snowy whiteness of the counterpane contrasted strangely with the bronzed, weather-beaten features and large, gnarled hands of the woman beneath, so like a mummy that her breathing alone seemed human.

Yet regular and warm as an infant's, her breath issued through her half-open mouth. No muscle stirred. No sound broke the silence; until, in the distance, floating above the orange groves, and on to the Christmas day, rang the bells of old San Gabriel.

# XII

A soothing peace possessed me, as I listened to the ringing of the old bells. I left quietly the bedside of the aged sleeper to kneel a moment later by that of my child. The healthy loveliness which I beheld completed my restoration. As I kissed the dainty, dimpled hands, and laid my cheek against the yellow curls, her warm, sweet breath infused my flagging circulation with the energy of love.

I no longer forgot my plans for the morning. Hastily dressing, I gathered as quickly as possible the various mysterious parcels secreted about my room, glancing occasionally at Marjorie to be sure that no possum slumbers hid beneath deceitful lashes. Satisfied that my schemes were unsuspected, I fled eagerly, with ladened arms, from the silent house out into the crisp, inspiring air of the sacred morning.

The sun was now well up. As it rose, it touched with magical radiance the most distant reaches of the Christmas landscape.

Reverently I lingered, enthralled with the breath of Judea. Standing beneath the old palms I listened to an anthem, led by a lark and sustained by the lowing cattle, who seemed to tell, as at first, the birth of the long-expected Saviour; while the rosebuds reflected from jeweled hearts his pure parables.

About me the purple mountains gleamed with the fresh, cool touch of the night. Between twin spurs, resting against the bosom of the sky, snow had gathered, until in the distant outline a pure, white lamb appeared, slain for the holy festival.

Old Baldy, the high priest of the morning, until now had withheld the fullness of his majesty. Suddenly the sun with golden shafts rent far asunder the misty veil that had enveloped his hoary summit. Transfigured with supernatural glory, the morning seemed to pause for one still moment, as if to receive his benediction.

"I, too, have been to the early celebration," I said to my heart, as I turned reluctantly to the pressing demands of the now inaugurated day.

Hastily I hid the packages in various secret nooks, while I decorated a great white rose tree with cornucopias and knicknacks.

Hardly had the last bauble been hung upon the magnificent Christmas tree when I heard the plaintive voice of my child.

I hurried to the house to find the little girl upon the bed, struggling bravely with her shoes and stockings.

"Did the fairies come?" she demanded, springing into my arms for her Christmas kiss.

For my answer I carried her to the window, through which she beheld the white rose tree.

"See," I said, "how good are the good little fairies to good little girls."

"May I go as soon as I am dressed and pick the tree?" the child besought, her eyes beaming with expectation.

"Yes," I said, "you may go, but I think the fairies would rather you would wait until our kind Doña Maria and Mariposilla return from church. The Doña Maria must be very weary; she has not slept all night for watching at the bedside of the grandmother. I think I know a little girl who might help to get breakfast, so that when the Doña Maria returns she can refresh herself at once with some hot coffee. I wonder if the little girl's name is Marjorie? Or perhaps I am mistaken; I may have forgotten her name."

Marjorie took one long, regretful look at the rose-tree; then from her baby heart there escaped a tragic little sigh that was half a sob. "Please, dear mamma," she said, bravely, "I will mind the fairies."

Fortunately for both mother and child, their resolution was not long tested.

It took but a few moments to prepare the toast and coffee, for Antonio had unexpectedly lighted the fire and filled the water kettle. Before our simple meal was quite ready the Doña Maria and Mariposilla had arrived.

It was amusing to witness the Doña Maria's mortification when she perceived that I had cooked the breakfast; her distress was genuine when she declared that the Señora would certainly be ill. "I am ashamed that I should have remained so long," she apologized. "The Señora should not have arisen until our return. It is ill fortune that she has not permitted me to prepare her a dainty holiday breakfast."

"Dear Doña Maria," I entreated, "why will you deplore what is already accomplished? I have told you often that a simple breakfast is all that I require, and our frolic has given me a fine appetite. See," I urged, "is my toast not a delicious brown? Make haste and enjoy the coffee, or I shall be greatly disappointed."

"The Señora is most kind," the Doña Maria replied, seating herself submissively. With her dark hand she brushed away a tear. "We are ever happy, my daughter and I, that we have known one so good and gentle," she added, feelingly.

Marjorie and Mariposilla had by this time declared it impossible to resist longer the fascinations of the rose-tree, tantalizingly visible through the open door. Gaining permission, they scampered away, followed by the hounds. The dogs appeared to understand the occasion. They ran forward, doubling over with excitement, as though expecting to find a jack-rabbit suspended from a bough of the Christmas tree. The picture was a pretty one, and none of us enjoyed it more than the Doña Maria, who soon left the table and joined the children in their merry hunt for the hidden parcels.

Marjorie led her about at will, compelling the sedate woman to stoop and caper as she had not done for years. When the gifts had all been discovered, we arranged them in rows upon the Bermuda grass, preparatory to the untying of strings and ribbons.

Marjorie's row was long and diversified, while Mariposilla declared that she had never before received so many gifts at one time.

"It is because we are so good," Marjorie explained; "for you know that fairies never bring presents to naughty children, only just stones and mud."

We all laughed as we continued our occupation each untying in turn a parcel marked with the name of the recipient and the good fairy who had been responsible for its safe delivery from the foot of Old Baldy.

With each discovery the air was flooded with shrieks of approval. Marjorie rejoiced over every little treasure, while Mariposilla embraced us excitedly at each happy surprise.

Even the Doña Maria grew artlessly gay, appearing to forget that the grandmother might soon awaken, to be cared for like an infant, and that Christmas was now but a colorless counterfeit of years past.

"Ah!" exclaimed the sympathetic mother, when Mariposilla held up for admiration a little silver bracelet; "it is almost like the happiness of the old days. Not the same; for the Spanish gave not gifts, but the good cheer is most sweet. I grieve," she continued, "that the Señora and my child should not have known those once glad days—now gone forever. Then, all went about from rancho to rancho, free from sorrow; always joyful in abundance. But the holiday is no more what it once was—so full of mirth and sweet enjoyment for both old and young; yet ever sacred, for none dared forget to go to the old church when the bells rang lovingly the birth of the Holy Child.

"Dear Señora," she continued, her dark eyes intensifying with awakening memories; "could you have seen the beauty of the old

Spanish life, then, with thy gentle heart, tears would now fall for those of us who are left."

With increasing melancholy she explained that her child refused to grieve for the departed glory of her family.

"I am often miserable when I remember how different I once felt, so full of joy and pride when I dreamed that my children would thank always the sweet Mother for the nobility of their father's name. Yet I blame not Mariposilla; for she saw not my husband, Don Arturo. Her life was too late to know of his goodness and beauty. I could forgive always her thoughtless indifference, if only sometimes she would weep when I show her the riding jacket embroidered with gold, and the botas of exceeding richness, once worn by her dear father. But she is cold, and understands not what she has lost. She would even profane the precious shawls of her grandmother, urging that some be sold to envious Americans for gold!"

Poor Doña Maria! I feared that her transient happiness had fled. But she soon controlled the dash of bitterness that tinctured for a moment her reminiscences, and continued to describe the wonderful days, once enjoyed by her now scattered and Americanized people.

"Think not, dear Señora, that I am ungrateful," she begged, sweetly. "It is perhaps best that my child should grow like the Americans. Her older kinsmen will soon be gone; the younger ones, like herself, care not to continue in the old way, seeking to marry with strangers, forgetting often even the religion of their childhood."

I was loath to interrupt the gentle complaints of the Doña Maria; for beneath the shadow of the venerable palms her sweet, low, sympathetic voice enthralled me with realistic glimpses of her picturesque past.

Tears dropped upon the brown cheeks when she told how she had knelt for the communion that same morning, alone with her child, surrounded no longer by dear, familiar faces.

"How different it once was!" she explained eagerly. "How sad, yet good, to remember how once the altar rail was thronged with near relatives and loving friends. To think how joyful were our hearts when we had received and could go absolved from the cold church into the warm sunshine, there to speak pleasant kind words and wish to each other a merry day. How beautiful to listen to the gay greetings of the young, to grasp the hands of dear ones, and hear, upon all sides, 'Feliz noche buena!'"

"Come," she said, rising; "my mother still sleeps, and I will show you the silken shawls, the lace mantillas, and the embroidered garments of our family."

Gladly I followed her to the little chamber, where she opened reverently a huge chest, from which she drew, one by one, the beautiful relics of her prosperity.

With loving care she took from scented wrappings gorgeous shawls of crêpe, blooming on both sides with rich, yet delicately wrought flowers, mantillas of wonderful lace, and dainty bits of Spanish finery, that brought to my lips repeated exclamations of wonder and delight.

"I am happy to have shown the Señora my treasures," she said, flushing with pleasure, as she drew, from a silken bag embroidered with silver, a scarf which she had reserved until the last, as the most precious and beautiful heirloom in her possession.

Draping it pathetically about her somber figure, she urged me to admire the delicate green which displayed so marvellously the butterflies embroidered in pink and gold, studded with real jewels.

"See!" she cried, caressing tenderly the clinging fabric; "is it not wonderful! So bright and sparkling after all the sad years!"

"The Señora will understand how dear is the scarf of the butterflies, when I relate to her its story, explaining how it came from Spain, the gift of my husband's grandmother; how I wore it to church upon our wedding day to shield from the sun the neck and arms that were once my foolish pride; how, when we were returning from our marriage, mounted upon horses decked with roses and splendid with silver and jewels, my husband, desirous that all should see the magnificence of my satin gown, caught away playfully the scarf, throwing it about his own shoulders, while he declared that all must behold the beauty of his bride. After a time, when our child was born, my husband brought again the scarf of the butterflies, commanding my mother to wrap it about our boy, that he might carry him upon the veranda to be admired by our assembled household.

"Ah! Señora, was not my husband proud the day he went with a company to the church for the christening of our child? Many relatives had arrived from Los Angeles and from Ventura, so that our house was overflowing with cheer. The kitchen and the court were gay with preparations from morning until evening. Although I could not go myself to the church, my husband told me joyfully how the dear old Father who had married us the year before took in his arms our boy, blessing him with double certainty when he kissed his little cheek.

"But too beautiful to live was our baby, and in one short year we gave him tearfully to the sweet Mother of Heaven, who heard not our prayers when our little one lay ill. Two more sons, grown almost to manhood, we lost; and then my brave husband, who had ever grieved sorely for his boys, went too.

"I alone remained with my mother and my unborn child, who came not until her father had been five months dead.

"See," she said, wiping away the tears that suffused her great, sad eyes; "see, dear Señora, the little petticoats of my dead babies, all now yellow with age.

"Who will care, when I am gone, for the worthless garments of my little ones? Surely not Mariposilla, for she understands not why I should still grieve, after the long years that have passed.

"She loves, however, the scarf of the butterflies, and begs often to possess it. When I am taken she may do as she desires with it, for it will then be her own, to treasure or to resign unto strangers.

"Yet I pray that she may always hold sacred the gift of her father's grandmother; for she, too, was carried to her christening wrapped in the beautiful shawl.

"Well do I remember how sore was my heart the day that my mother went alone to the church with my fatherless child. So ill was I, that I cared not even to name my little daughter, entreating my mother to consult with the priest, who might choose for us.

"But my good mother was wiser than I, and when she had thought much she remembered the butterflies upon the beautiful scarf, and how my husband, Don Arturo, had delighted to behold them glistening in the sunlight when I first wore the shawl to my bridal; how, afterwards, he insisted that his children should first be shown to his household wrapped in the splendid gift of his grandmother. Wisely she remembered these things, and when, weeks after, I asked her the name of my child, I wept for joy when she said, 'She is Mariposilla.'"

Tenderly the dark hand folded and replaced in its embroidered bag the precious scarf of the butterflies. Tearfully she laid it away by the side of the sparkling riding-jacket and gorgeous botas of the dead Arturo, while she reverently closed the old chest, relegating to its scented depths the fading remnants of her former grandeur, together with the sad, sweet memories of her poetic life.

# XIII

It had been arranged that we should go to San Gabriel late in the afternoon of Christmas Day.

As the time approached for our departure, I grew more reluctant to leave the ranch. I was still loath to submit to the restraints of a hotel. Had I dared, I would have abandoned the visit. It irritated me to submit heroically to exile from Paradise, but there now seemed no alternative.

The little valise had been packed for hours; the precious evening frock safely folded away in its scented wrappings, together with little bits of finery to be worn at the hotel. Mariposilla, radiant and expectant, counted the moments which delayed our departure.

Even the grandmother was now comfortably restored, having awakened from her long sleep fresh and docile.

No vestige of excuse remained to justify a change in our plans. An ordained agreement of trifles appeared conspiring with Fate.

As we bade farewell to the Doña Maria, I found it impossible to resist the unhappy presentiments which thronged our departure.

When we drove away with Sidney and passed between the great century plants, a sudden fear seized my vacillating will. I knew in an instant that I dreaded the possible consequences of what I had undertaken.

In the front seat of the trap, with Sidney, sat Mariposilla, transformed by excessive happiness and conventional garb into another creature. Never again would she be the child she had been even that same morning, when she had romped upon the Bermuda grass with Marjorie, flushed with pleasure over her Christmas trifles. Now another flush was upon her cheeks, another light shone in her eyes; for, even as I looked, Mariposilla had bidden farewell forever to the restraints of her simple, beautiful childhood.

Had I created a scene by turning back in our journey into the world, it is hardly possible that I could have obviated the difficulties of Mariposilla's emancipation from the life she had determined to escape.

As I continued to face the responsibilities of her case I grew more tranquil. I reasoned that it was perhaps best not to resist the unmistakable leadings of Fate, which seemed to point to a destiny for the girl different from the one desired by the Doña Maria. Her remarkable beauty, the truly good blood which ran in her veins, to say nothing of her laudable ambition and determination not to accept a husband dictated by the priest or her relatives, justified me in the belief that she had outgrown the old life, which was now each day growing more and more intolerable.

With care and advantages, it seemed not only credible, but certain, that Mariposilla might eventually satisfy her ambition.

The longer I thought upon the subject, the more I felt it to be my duty to watch jealously the marvelous and unavoidable development of this wonderful girl.

In a word, I compromised with my contending emotions, instituting myself the guardian of her glorious beauty. Our arrival at the hotel was concurrent with the usual lively glimpses of festivity always prevalent at a pleasure resort upon the approach of evening. A gush of music, the ripple of laughter, the tripping of feet, and the spontaneous rush of cherubs in white frocks to investigate our arrival constituted for Mariposilla and Marjorie a prime reception.

Mrs. Sanderson awaited us upon the landing of the broad staircase, then led us cordially to her own apartments. When she threw open the door to her sitting-room, Mariposilla exclaimed with pleasure as the lady drew her affectionately to the open fire.

"Sit down, little one," she said. "I will draw some tea, while Sid attends to the luggage. My pretty butterfly must be warmed after her drive; for of course she is to outshine all beauties at the ball to-night."

As Mrs. Sanderson spoke, she went to the tea-table, where the kettle was already singing.

I could see, as Mariposilla received her tea from the hand of our hostess, that the shell-like cup and saucer were a source of apprehension. The child dreaded a catastrophe more than she would have dreaded, a month previous, a dire calamity in her family.

Covertly she watched me as I deposited upon the side of my saucer the biscuit that must not interfere with the manipulation of my spoon.

But, although she endeavored to follow my exact policy, her first attempt at tea drinking was destined to be unfortunate.

Mariposilla had not yet achieved the confidence necessary for the poise and counterpoise of the treacherous spoon. The girl had not yet attained the dallying point. She could not yet sip tea one moment with assurance, the next, disregard the responsibilities of Dresden or Coalport china while she chatted unconsciously with her neighbor.

Notwithstanding her most earnest efforts to succeed in the undertaking, the spoon flew at an aggravating tangent across the room. In a frantic lurch to capture it she upset her cup, spilling into her lap the steaming tea.

In a moment Mrs. Sanderson was by her side.

"Dear child," she said, sympathetically, relieving the girl at once from her costly incumbrances. "I alone am to blame for offering you that stupid cup. Sid declares each time it is used that it shall be the last.

"You see," she added charmingly, "those miserable little feet, that look so secure when the cup is standing upon the saucer, have a malicious way of running away. They are just like the profligate dish that eloped with the spoon, when the cow jumped over the moon."

In a moment, Mariposilla had forgotten her embarrassment.

The lady took her at once to her bedroom, where she sponged away the stains, petting and reassuring the child until she glowed with happiness.

Soon Sidney came to say that our rooms were ready, urging us, as we withdrew, not to be late for dinner.

When we had unpacked our apparel, Mariposilla became at once absorbed in the delights of her toilet, speculating innocently, while she dressed, in regard to the mysteries of the cotillion, which she was to witness for the first time after dinner.

The cream and gold frock was joyfully assumed, and if possible the girl's pleasure was keener than upon the previous evening.

With true womanly instinct she established the harmonious intimacy between herself and her finery which at first had been lacking. She now wore her gown with composure. None would have suspected that she had not always been well dressed.

She had pushed above the elbow the wide, puffy sleeves, displaying the lower half of her rounded arms; while the smile that parted her lips told plainly of satisfaction, when she regarded the effect.

Now that her mother was absent she wore fearlessly the shining bracelet. About her throat she fastened with delighted vanity the little necklace, declaring, with one more loving glance into the mirror, that she was ready.

Marjorie, having finished her tea, had obediently retired, satisfied to watch for a few moments from her bed our elaborate preparations. She was deeply moved by our grand toilets, pronouncing us "the beautifulest peoples in the house." I was the loveliest of mammas, in my long neglected "dwaggin dress"; while upon Mariposilla she bestowed a profusion of compliments, as pretty as they were genuine.

When we had kissed the little girl good night, we started at once to rejoin our friends. Half way down the hall we met Mrs. Sanderson and her son coming to us.

The lady wore a rich lavender evening gown, while Sidney for the first time appeared before Mariposilla in the immaculate perfection of full dress.

I saw in a moment that the Spanish child was in an ecstasy of adoration. Ever after, it would be useless for the Doña Maria to endeavor to interest her in the magnificence of her father's once splendid apparel.

Even upon the threshold of this new experience she was captivated beyond release. Never again would she submit to her old life.

The next moment was felicitous, when Mrs. Sanderson took caressingly her hand. Drawing it within her own she commanded her son to escort us to dinner.

# XIV

As we disposed ourselves about the friendly table in the cheerful dining room, I could see that Mariposilla's wildest desires were at last realized.

She was trembling slightly, I fancied, as I glanced at her from my opposite position, but in a moment she had controlled herself, and if the ordeal of dinner had at first appeared formidable, she soon forgot her fears in rapturous happiness.

As upon the occasion of the Waltons' luncheon, she watched intelligently my every move, making no mistakes, as she received prettily the flattering attentions of those about her.

As dinner proceeded, the girl's excitement was manifest only in her transcendent coloring. She was dropping naturally, as well as gracefully, into the most difficult requirements of her social novitiate. As I watched her anxiously, I grew tranquil with the assurance that the first step in her education had been successfully taken, exulting, as I reflected upon the complications of modern dining.

One of my pet theories had led me to believe that I could discern correctly the character or native refinement of anyone, provided I could observe, unsuspected, his gastronomical endeavors. I had often discovered inherent resemblances to the brute, or lingering traces of the savage, as I watched covertly the table attainments of a person who, under other ordinary conditions, appeared eminently correct. I felt willing to stake extensive odds that Mariposilla's social success would progress satisfactorily in intelligent ratio to her first unique acquirement.

Our coffee was served in Mrs. Sanderson's sitting-room, where we were joined by a bevy of young people, to whom we were introduced in anticipation of the week's festivities.

Sidney and a young Englishman prepared to smoke, while the girls gathered about Mrs. Sanderson, like moths around a candle.

"Have you heard of the coincidence?" demanded Mrs. Wilbur, a dashing blonde, who thus far in the season had monopolized the attentions of the social leader's son. "Imagine, if you please, a shortage of young women for our cotillion."

"Just think of an extra man in San Gabriel!" shouted the girls in chorus; while Mrs. Wilbur appealed confidentially to Mrs. Sanderson to settle the impending difficulty.

"We were expecting six couples from Pasadena, and now, at the last moment, Ethel Walton sends word that the giddy widow who was to have chaperoned her party is ill, obliging them to bring a maiden lady who doesn't dance," she exclaimed.

"Delightful!" exclaimed the girls. "How jolly to boast a rover, and dear Mr. Eastman at that."

"Won't he be popular?" Mrs. Wilbur added, aside to Mrs. Sanderson, who was at that moment glancing interrogatively at Sidney.

The young man divined his mother's signal, for he came to her side with unusual alacrity.

"The very thing," the lady replied to his earnest undertone. "The arrangement will be quite proper, and I am sure that Mrs. Wilbur will relinquish you for Mr. Eastman. Won't you, my dear?" the lady continued, turning suddenly to Mrs. Wilbur, who was now beginning to suspect that Sidney was quite satisfied to obey the suggestion of his mother.

"It will be so interesting to watch Mariposilla dance in the cotillion," Mrs. Sanderson pursued, bravely. "Dear Mrs. Wilbur will excuse you, for my sake, I am sure, Sid," she added, sweetly, as she turned from that somewhat ruffled young woman to the Spanish child, who was prettily pleading her ignorance of cotillions.

"Never mind, dear," she said, coaxingly, to the timid girl, "you dance divinely, and Sid will take you through the figures beautifully."

I saw that Mrs. Wilbur was chagrined and angry, for a hot flush had dyed her cheeks, when she replied that of course Mr. Sanderson could do as he chose. As far as she was concerned she would be greatly pleased to dance with Mr. Eastman, having formerly refused him her partnership on account of an early engagement with Mr. Sanderson.

"My mother appears to have solved our difficulties. Mr. Eastman certainly surpasses me as a partner, and as there is no robbery in a beneficial exchange, with Mrs. Wilbur's permission, I will dance with Miss Del Valle," the young man responded, indifferently.

A suppressed titter from one of the girls had the unfortunate tendency to increase Mrs. Wilbur's pique.

She answered curtly that certainly Mrs. Sanderson had the first claim upon her son. "Mr. Eastman is a delightful partner, and I am exceptionally favored in the cut," she added, with spirit.

"Why, Mrs. Wilbur," exclaimed a girl with baby-blue eyes and a sympathetic costume, embellished by infant devices; "how dare you perpetrate a pun? You are surely not ignorant of the punishment which fits such a crime?"

"While you, my dear, have yet to learn of penalties arranged for young women who can not distinguish between a pun and a simile," Mrs. Wilbur replied.

Mrs. Sanderson, perceiving that the air was becoming tinctured with personalities, declared that there were also penalties for being disagreeable.

"Come," she said, "let us resist the desire to quarrel. I am sure that Mrs. Wilbur and Sidney are both satisfied, they have simply been misunderstood; and under the circumstances it becomes a polite duty to change the subject."

As the lady finished her tactful and decisive rejoinder, she took from the table a package which had just arrived by express from New York.

"A box of chocolate creams for the one who guesses my Christmas gift," she said, graciously, holding above the throng a long, narrow package, that was certainly not suggestive of any particular thing.

"Each person shall have three guesses, which Mrs. Wilbur will kindly record."

"Go, Sid, and fetch some paper," his mother commanded; turning sweetly to Mrs. Wilbur, who was evidently weighing the consequences of refusing to act as secretary.

However, when Mr. Sanderson brought the writing pad and pencil she accepted them with mollified mien.

"Mr. Brooke shall guess first," Mrs. Sanderson said, addressing the diminutive Englishman, who was smoking before the fire.

"What do you say my package contains, Mr. Brooke?" the lady urged; when the young man persisted in a grinning silence.

"Weally, my deah lady, I am deucid poor at a fancy;" he at length divulged.

"Never mind," cried the aggressive baby girl; "say anything! Time is precious."

"As you insist," the man replied, "I fancy the package contains Mr. Sanderson's sweetheart."

"That is but one guess," objected Mrs. Wilbur, "there are two more possibilities in store for you."

"Three sweethearts, as you bother so," the Englishman replied, greatly elated at his wit.

"Very well," said Mrs. Sanderson. "Three sweethearts are surely not an impossibility to a young man; are they, Sid?"

"Certainly not," her son replied, as he lit, with adorable indifference, a fresh cigar.

"Now, my little Butterfly shall guess," Mrs. Sanderson declared, turning to Mariposilla, who was the unconscious center of the admiring throng. All listened eagerly to hear what the beautiful child would say; suffused as she was with charming embarrassment.

"I am sure it is a gift of devotion and great affection," she answered modestly, gazing with touching earnestness into the face of her adored friend.

"How extremely pretty!" approved Mrs. Sanderson.

"Thus far the contents of the package is enchantingly abstract; can not some one, who is matter-of-fact, indulge in a guess which is tangible?"

In accordance with the request, there followed in quick succession a volley of reckless ventures, each outdoing the other in substantial reality.

When the guessing ceased, Mrs. Wilbur remarked the weight of the package, and announced that she believed the box contained shot. "Nothing but lead could weigh so heavily, but of course, as secretary, I am not guessing," she remarked, indifferently.

"Surely, you must guess!" Mrs. Sanderson urged, sweetly; but as Mrs. Wilbur insisted that she preferred to keep out of the game, the lady said no more, but proceeded to undo the mysterious parcel.

A shout of admiration burst from the expectant company when she exposed for view an elegant silver picture shrine, containing three superb postures of a beautiful girl.

"By Jove, I am right!" lisped the Rivulet, gleefully. "Did I not say three sweethearts?"

"Certainly Mr. Brooke has won," several cried at once.

"Don't be so sure," retorted Mrs. Wilbur, in an undertone. "Did I not say the box contained shot? If you doubt the fact, look at the Spanish girl," she added, censoriously, to Sidney, who appeared not to hear.

It was true that Mariposilla had grown strangely pale. She seemed like one smitten by a remorseless blast. Instinctively she vanished from Mrs. Sanderson's side, while her pitiful eyes implored me to take her away.

Fortunately, at this particular time the tallyho arrived from Pasadena, and to my infinite joy the situation was relieved. Mariposilla, forgotten in the excitement, soon regained her composure, and later, when we entered the ballroom, her color was restored and her distress obliterated.

I was glad that Mrs. Wilbur and I had alone witnessed the child's jealousy. The rest of the company had been too busy admiring the pictures to notice Mariposilla's pale countenance; while Mrs. Wilbur's sarcasms had been uttered low, apart from the throng, as she sat by the table on which she had been writing.

I felt that the poor child's secret was safe for this evening, at least; for I believed Mrs. Wilbur too wily to acknowledge her rival at present. The woman of the world still hoped to distance the Spanish child.

I could see that she was determined to drive her to a disadvantage if possible.

The cotillion was not to be enjoyed until a programme of dances had been offered to all the guests of the hotel, some of whom had not been favored with invitations for the cotillion.

This arrangement proved fortunate for Mariposilla. She forgot her first slight embarrassment entirely, as she glided happily among the less exclusive throng, who good-naturedly jostled her as she passed in the dance.

Sidney had assumed entire charge of her. He had arranged her programme with great consideration, interspersing his own name freely between the names of the most desirable men in the room; while he reserved for himself the privilege of escorting her to the refreshment room, preparatory to the cotillion.

The evening from its beginning appeared auspicious for Mariposilla. Between dances the child flitted to my side like a happy bird.

"It is most grand, Señora!" she whispered, as Sidney drew her away for a waltz.

During refreshments, I noticed that Mrs. Wilbur was both fascinated and annoyed at the sensation the girl was producing. Where would the matter end? I asked myself.

Even in the midst of Mariposilla's apparent success, I felt my heart sinking with apprehension. "Why," I questioned, "Why did I let her come?"

The dancers were rapidly leaving the supper room, and when I looked for Mariposilla, she, too, had disappeared. Thinking that she had gone below into the ball-room, I followed hastily; but she was not there. Excusing myself to Mrs. Sanderson, upon the plea that I must peep at Marjorie, I ran hastily above, hoping to find my charge in one of the reception rooms. Faithfully I searched the parlors and corridors, and later the verandas, in vain, for a trace of the truants, so successfully escaping me.

There was yet Mrs. Sanderson's sitting-room. I must pass it on the way to Marjorie.

I hastily ascended the stairs, contemplating, as I flew along the hall, my chances of interrupting a tête-a-tête.

I felt indignant that Sidney Sanderson should abuse so soon my confidence.

I realized that Mariposilla already had been missed by her rival, and the thought that the inexperienced child would doubtless be criticised, and perhaps maligned, was decidedly irritating.

Slackening my pace as I approached the vicinity of Mrs. Sanderson's parlor, I perceived the door ajar. A second more and I comprehended the absurdity of my vigilant endeavors. My conscientious plans and sentimental reservations, thus far, were not proving superior to the wiles of Cupid.

I winced cruelly when I remembered the confident schemes for Mariposilla's gradual translation into the bosom of the conventional world.

In the center of the room, her profile outlined by acute emotion, stood the Spanish girl. Bending beside her, Sidney was evincing an ardency entirely paradoxical, when I considered his indifferent temperament.

Mariposilla held in her hands, which trembled, the silver shrine, containing the pictures of the beautiful girl.

"You love her not?" she repeated in an ecstasy of doubt; her voice gradually rising in joy at the sweet denial she had forced from the lips of her lover.

Her head was still in profile, but the long lashes, that had lifted to disclose her rapture, now dropped like a sable fringe upon her precious secret, while she listened in silent contentment to the deep undertone assurances of the man by her side.

I could endure the restraint no longer. Tapping deceitfully upon the door, I began at once an animated search for my fan, inwardly disgusted with my cowardice, furious over my imbecile failure as a chaperone.

# XV

Mariposilla was the belle of the cotillion. Seated between Sidney and Ethel Walton, she knew no embarrassment. When dancing, she was absolutely free from self-consciousness.

I assisted Mrs. Sanderson at the favor tables, where I had every opportunity of observing the girl's behavior.

She was constantly called out, and to my delight accepted her popularity with gracious modesty.

Often, when she came for a favor, Mrs. Sanderson delayed her to whisper a compliment, or else to lavish upon her a marked caress.

From first to last, the happy child was noticeably bedecked with trophies of success. In her hair a number of gauzy butterflies of different hues fluttered as she danced, encouraging the fancy that she was truly related to the gorgeous little creatures after which she had been named.

By the side of the Spanish child the other girls appeared artificial. Their respective claims to beauty seemed easily determined, the limit of their fascinations soon estimated.

"I never felt so blasé in my life before," Ethel Walton whispered, as I handed her a favor. Later, when there was an intermission in the cotillion, she crossed the room and sat by my side.

"As I told you once, I feel dreadfully blasé to-night," she said, picking to pieces a rose which had fallen away from her stylish gown. "To watch your wonderful protégée rejoicing over the sweet, uncertain trophies of her first cotillion, is entirely refreshing. Her extravagant happiness makes me feel as though I had finished my course and been decidedly beaten."

"Did you ever see anyone so effulgent?" Ethel continued, following with her eyes the outlines of Mariposilla's figure. "No one in the room can approach her in beauty," she mused amiably. "And yet the girl inspires no jealousy; for, like Donatello, her moral nature seems absolutely undeveloped. Sometimes she seems like an exquisite link between nature and the fallen angels."

"Have you, too, noticed this?" I exclaimed.

"Yes," Ethel replied, "I have been thinking about her ever since that first visit to Crown Hill. If I am ever famous in the Salon, Mariposilla shall be the theme for my picture."

"If you work I am sure you will succeed," I replied.

"I hope I shall continue to work," she answered, "but even work is an uncertain proviso. Sometimes I wonder why God inconveniences the ordinary mortal with an imagination. Why does he not reserve the allurements of art for the genius of the century alone?"

"I so often envy my sister," the girl continued. "It is beautiful to watch her at a high church service. This one exalted caprice seems to satisfy entirely her cravings after the extraordinary. She believes the tenets of her faith so implicitly that she is never beguiled into uncomfortable doubts. She never reaches after unattainable things, and is absolutely satisfied with the common conventions of life."

"Then surely she is happy?" I replied.

"Yes," answered Ethel, "but look at Sidney Sanderson. Certainly he is in love with Mariposilla! Watch him a moment and see how he has forgotten his blasé part to-night. All things considered, I believe the match would be a good one," she continued. "Sid is carnal enough to appreciate Mariposilla's physical perfection, and I believe he could easily dispense with moral and intellectual qualities."

Later, when Ethel bade me good-night, she whispered that I might depend upon her as my ally. "If Mr. Sidney becomes too masterful let me know," she said, gaily, as she enveloped herself in the folds of her evening cloak.

Long after the hotel had been hushed with the final hush which follows a ball, I lay awake thinking of Mariposilla and the possible intentions of Sidney Sanderson. Time after time her beautiful, passionate face appeared before me, tortured, one moment, with wild, half-civilized jealousy; the next, transcendent with blissful trust in the man she loved.

When I awoke from my unrefreshing slumbers at the usual time, aroused by Marjorie, who had crawled into my bed, I felt that I must invent a pretext for returning Mariposilla as soon as possible to the care of her mother.

The morning was dull. A prophetic contrast to the glorious Christmas dawn of the day before. The rains had been threatening at intervals for several weeks, but the sun had dissipated the clouds each day, leaving always the impression of a pleasant trick arranged for the bewildered tourist, who, contrary to the example of natives and adopted Californians, lugged about persistently his mackintosh and umbrella, declaring each cloudy morning that rain must certainly fall before night. Then, suddenly, the gray clouds seemed to melt into the liquid blue of the sky, while against the sides of the purple mountains only one long streak of vapor rested, like the shroud of a giant.

The week before Christmas the sky had smoothed away its every trace of rain. Light snows had sugared the feathery outlines of the distant peaks, and the delighted tourist had hung up his mackintosh and umbrella, deciding that the climates of Southern France and Italy were not to be considered with that of Southern California. Now the clouds had returned reënforced. The range had grown richer in color, almost black, except when the sun shot for a moment his presence in temporary triumph against a spur, that glistened responsively, while the cañons scowled in dark disapproval. Then, all at once, a gloom, like a half-dropped curtain, settled back of the foothills, defying the prophecies of the most ancient mariner of the Coast.

As I awoke I felt with unusual depression the absence of the sun. And when I drew aside my curtains I peered in vain for streaks of gold threading the horizon. The morning was lifeless and gray. Even the great clusters of cactus, the remains of the natural wall planted by the good padres years ago for protection against the Indians, seemed an invasion of gray spirits. Not so when the sun glanced their bristling tops, for then they shone like knights in full armor.

My heart went out in childish homesickness to the Doña Maria and the little nest I had prepared for myself in her simple Spanish home. While I dressed myself and Marjorie, I turned over and over the subject which had taken possession of my thoughts. How could I escape the complications of this inopportune visit? How could I, without offending the Sandersons and noticeably meddling with the discretion of the Doña Maria, return quietly with Mariposilla to the ranch?

But the problem grew more difficult as the day advanced, for Mariposilla was now in a seventh heaven, which surpassed entirely her expectations. All at once she was the pet and sensation of the hotel. Mrs. Wilbur had conquered her pique of the previous evening, and, for reasons clear to herself, she flattered and patronized the child with unlooked-for benevolence. The gay young woman seemed to have recovered her lost temper, for she urged Sidney and Mariposilla to waltz after breakfast, volunteering, with sweet unselfishness, to furnish the music for the aimless crowd who had congregated in the ball-room. Later, the tennis experts insisted on a few last sets before the rain, and all sauntered in the direction of the courts, pairing off as they went, drawn by the flirtatious affinities of the moment.

However, tennis soon languished, and the crowd returned to the Sandersons' sitting-room to beguile the rest of the morning with guitars and banjos. Mrs. Wilbur professed unbounded admiration for Mariposilla's performances, and engaged to practice with her that same afternoon, when the present audience had dispersed for beauty naps.

"We could soon play together wonderfully well," she declared. The woman had evidently decided that her best game was to patronize Mrs. Sanderson's guest, if she intended to regain the attentions of Sidney when the girl departed. Yet she loved to embitter the latent apprehensions of the poor child by constant reference to the face in the silver shrine. I could see that although Mariposilla carried herself with unusual composure, there was beneath her stifling calm a lurking tempest of doubt and jealousy. She seemed horribly fascinated by the unpleasant possibilities of the beautiful face that occupied so many conspicuous situations in the room. She gazed again and again at the lovely, aristocratic features which haunted her to despair. Once she locked them passionately in their silver case. Quickly turning to a pile of music, she tried to hide her secret; but Mrs. Sanderson had observed her.

"Looking at my beautiful Gladys again?" she said, drawing the blushing child to her side. "I hope you will know her some day, for Gladys would love you dearly. She adores everything beautiful."

The color deepened beneath the Spanish girl's cheek as Sidney's mother continued to explain the tender relations existing between herself and the New York heiress.

"Gladys is the daughter of a school friend, who died when her little one was but six years old. She is my godchild, and I have watched the motherless child grow up, thinking always of her loss. The dear girl has many lovers, but refuses them all. She lives only for her father, who is an invalid. She will never marry, I am afraid, during his life. I had hoped to bring them both to California, but, instead, they have gone to a sanatorium, about which Gladys has grown quite wild. The poor girl believes that her father is going to recover, and has shut herself away from society and friends, only to be disappointed," the lady added, with calculating sympathy.

"Perhaps her father will live many years," Mariposilla said, eagerly. To the suspicious child no Providential arrangement could be more satisfactory. That the father of Gladys might be spared to a green old age would now become a part of her prayers. She would say, that very evening, a double number of aves to our dear Lady. She would supplicate her to keep the beautiful Gladys with her father in the hospital for many years. Then, perhaps—she told her poor, foolish, jealous little heart—then, perhaps, Sidney would love only herself.

# XVI

For a brief period in the afternoon the clouds of the morning promised to disperse. The wind shifted from the rain quarter, and the sun made a sickly attempt to shine.

Patches of yellow light tantalized the sulky sides of the mountains. A presumptuous rainbow started to span the sky, but parted in the middle and soon disappeared in the settled gloom which quickly followed.

When the sun first tried to break through the clouds, shortly after luncheon, Mrs. Sanderson proposed a walk.

"Come," she said, "I must have the air. One can not house up in California. Even one day indoors stifles. Mariposilla has arranged to practice duets with Mrs. Wilbur. Sid is obliged to go to Los Angeles; Marjorie is asleep. Our best plan is to walk down to the Mission and back."

We had gone but half way to the old church when we perceived that a rain storm was now indeed coming. Each moment the air grew colder. The wind suddenly ceased to compromise with the south, changing almost immediately into the east. The mountains disappeared, and soon the foothills were hidden beneath a smooth veil of mist. Several immense drops announced the gathering downpour.

"Come," said Mrs. Sanderson, "let us make haste, before we are drenched."

We were both famous pedestrians, yet before we had reached the hotel the rain was pelting our faces with stinging persistency. We barely reached the veranda when the deluge came.

Those who have seen a California rainstorm, watching for days, perhaps weeks, the baffled efforts of the clouds to wipe out the landscape, will understand the term. No word but "deluge" describes adequately the steady, unremitting torrent which breaks at last from the sky.

As we entered the house I felt like crying. I was chilly and tired, and had the feeling that I had been beaten even by Nature. There was now no excuse for returning to the ranch until after the rain. I had foolishly pleaded the danger of exposing Marjorie to the drive, in case of a storm, and now the rain had come—come to stay for several days; perhaps for a week. I could not consistently depart until the downpour had ceased.

When I said early in the day to Mrs. Sanderson that the weather had become so threatening that I would very much prefer taking the

MARY STEWART DAGGETT

children home, she silenced me by reminding me that Mariposilla was visiting with the full consent of the Doña Maria.

"The child would be heart-broken to lose one day of her promised week. As for yourself, you need a change to wake you up. It is absurd for one so young to refuse the natural enjoyments of youth, and I think your determination not to dance a pretty but silly affectation. California is not the place to mourn in. The climate is opposed to dejection. The natives go to funerals in the morning and chase with the hounds in the afternoon."

"Don't," I cried peremptorily. "Don't make me believe that you mean what you say."

"All the same, I do," she replied. "I am a fatalist, and while I am permitted to enjoy myself, I shall avoid sackcloth and ashes."

Perceiving that I was hurt, she endeavored to appease me.

"Never mind, little dignity," she said, smiling her rarest smile. "You are always preaching me silent sermons; though you don't mean to scorn me, I feel your principle in the air, until I am wild to shock you in return."

Later, we went for our walk, each a little uncomfortable, as each began to wonder why she had chosen the other for her friend.

Upon our return Mrs. Sanderson had remained in the corridor in front of the open fire attempting to dry her dress. I went above at once. As I passed the familiar sitting-room I saw through the open door that the room was deserted. Mrs. Wilbur and Mariposilla had evidently not made a success of the practicing. Without stopping I went to my own rooms, where I found Marjorie still asleep.

Pushing open a communicating door, I saw Mariposilla upon her bed. Her head was buried in the pillow, while long, choking sobs caught and held her breath. She had been so happy but a short time before, flattered and pleased because Mrs. Wilbur had invited her to practice duets, that I was surprised at her condition.

"Tell me, dear child," I said, gently, "what has happened."

For several moments she refused to speak, but after a time she grew more composed. It was clear to me at once that Mrs. Wilbur was responsible for the girl's passionate grief.

"Never mind my unhappiness, dear Señora," she said at last, touchingly. "I am a poor, foolish girl, and must weep when I am sad; just as I rejoice when I am happy. It is not so with the Americans—they smile always, even though they are miserable."

I found it impossible to insist upon a confidence.

"Yes, dear," I agreed, "as people grow wise and worldly, they generally grow deceitful. I dare not advise you to cultivate insincerity; but for convenience you must endeavor to control your emotions. You will, after a time, learn that it is often best to smile, even though you feel sore. Often a heartache or a heart hunger will go away when we have bravely concealed it."

"Indeed, I have done so!" she cried, fiercely. Rising from the bed she confronted me excitedly. Upon her sweet face, still wet with tears, there was an exultant expression, mingled with tragic distress.

"She knew not that I was unhappy! She thought only to make me wretched, but I wept not until I was alone," she sobbed, triumphantly.

Poor little one! how my heart ached for her! How readily was she acquiring the miserable experience from which I would have saved her. Never again could she be the Mariposilla she had been before this unfortunate visit.

The flame was now lighted which threatened to consume her.

"Come, dear," I said; "you must not mind Mrs. Wilbur. She is a vain, foolish woman. If she has hurt your feelings, she has shown herself coarse and vulgar. Perhaps we had better order a close carriage and go back to the dear Doña Maria," I continued, jumping at the opportunity to escape from our difficult surroundings.

"No, no!" she cried, passionately; "let us not go away. I will be foolish no more. I will look no more into the silver shrine if only we may stay longer."

It was impossible to repulse her confidence. I could not then urge her to shield her love from the probabilities of disappointment. I could not add to the anguish of her afternoon. I shrank from assisting Mrs. Wilbur in her cowardly attack. At present I must wait. A few days, at most, would restore the child to the care of her mother. I would then know better what course to pursue.

In my inmost heart I believed that Sidney Sanderson would be willing to marry the beautiful Spanish girl, but as yet I could not interpret his mother.

I was beginning to feel more and more the woman's artful depth, but yet I did not really doubt her.

Mariposilla was now quite composed; the thought of our return to the ranch had silenced her at once. She bathed her face and dressed for dinner with the greatest care, soon appearing as if nothing had occurred to disturb her.

In defiance to the pelting rain, an impromptu dance was arranged for the evening.

After dinner the young people flew to their rooms to improvise fancy costumes, for Mrs. Sanderson had decided that the ball should be masqué.

The lady showed at once great energy in arranging the costumes to be worn by Mariposilla and Sidney. After considerable maneuvering, she succeeded in converting her son into a splendid Spanish cavalier. She had upon her wall a superb trophy of a sombrero, ornate with silver decorations, which, with other trifles and a red silk scarf properly arranged, completed the gallant don of the past. Mariposilla, in her actual character of sweet señorita, was enveloped in a rich mantilla of black lace, coquettishly caught upon the shoulders and to the hair with pink roses. A short black satin petticoat displayed the pretty little feet, encased in dainty slippers that shone with jeweled buckles. The girl's bare arms and hands glittered with the contents of Mrs. Sanderson's jewel box.

We all confessed that we had never seen anyone more beautiful. The theatrical yet natural character which she assumed had driven away every vestige of her depression. Never before had the child appeared so gay. Mrs. Wilbur's most insinuating remark had now no sting. The joyous present was enough; she would not believe that the future might be full of tears.

I remembered, long afterwards, how Sidney Sanderson had forgotten to look bored; and how both he and Mariposilla had neglected everyone in the room but each other, like two happy children in their devotion.

Not once again while we remained in the hotel did I see a shadow upon Mariposilla's brow. In vain did Mrs. Wilbur endeavor to excite her jealousy. The child was too happy to doubt. Each moment she grew more beautiful, maturing almost as we watched her, with the ripening influences of her strong first love.

# XVII

The breath of Easter was in the air. It was hard, even in that last penitential week, to renounce the seductive wooings of those first April days. In the little Episcopal chapel, or in the venerable Mission, we acknowledged each evening our infirmities; but with all our abnegation, there was for some of us an heterodox satisfaction in hastening away from our prayers.

We wanted to exult, rather than to bemoan "our manifold sins and wickedness."

We were not sufficiently impressed with our depravity to smell brimstone, when the air was richly purified with the scent of orange blossoms and millions of newborn roses.

Doubtless our lenten orthodoxy would have developed more strongly in the cutting blast of a Manitoba blizzard. We would have felt more contrite, drawn by the persuasive chastisements of a sweet spring cyclone. But in such days as the ones which followed each other like glad birds in a flock, it was difficult to assume a despondency adequate to the penitential demand.

The Gold of Ophir rose and Mariposilla were now blooming together. The old house was bright, outside and in, with light and glory.

From the veranda and the crest of the roof, long sprays of dazzling bloom swept voluptuously to the sky. In the blushing hearts of myriads of buds and blossoms, the sun whispered each day his rapturous secrets.

Wonderful from its first hour of triumph until its last pale, dilapidated petals have fallen to the ground—a moral to its transient magnificence—this rose is tragic.

It seems always the glorious prototype of Mariposilla, who ever stole its fickle lights and shades. As I watched, through those eventful weeks, the marvelous unfolding of bud to flower and child to maiden, I was never able to separate them in my thoughts. Their analogy was captivating.

I have already said that I learned instinctively to watch for the girl's mood in the complexion of the rose. When the edges of its petals burned with fire, I knew that Mariposilla, too, glowed with hope and ecstasy. When the fog smote sullenly the golden heart of the Ophir, I felt without looking that the girl, too, was pale, tortured with jealousy, and indefinite forebodings. Thus for me there will always remain the fancy that between this rose and the Spanish child there existed a kinship—a subtle sympathy, that each unconsciously felt when the other was near.

Looking back over those happy days, they seem fraught with no ordinary conditions. Unconsciously all took part in the several acts of a realistic drama.

I see now, as I could not then see, the innumerable cues, the important by-play and scenic situations, which eventually led up to an inevitable climax.

As the weeks glided away, I no longer doubted Sidney Sanderson's love for Mariposilla. Had there been a sign of opposition on the part of his mother, I would have warned the Doña Maria. But, to the contrary, Mrs. Sanderson increased her affection daily for her pretty plaything; often alluding to the girl's beneficial influence upon her son.

"The scamp is head and ears in love!" she said one day. "Just look at him. I should die of rage and jealousy if I didn't adore his sweetheart myself," she confided.

Mariposilla and Sidney were at the far end of the veranda, oblivious to all but each other.

The woman then went as far as to intimate that a few years in a fashionable New York school would do all that was necessary for Mariposilla.

"Beauty such as hers would be ruined by rigorous education. Fortunately, Sid hates wise women. Imagine Mariposilla developing the occult transitions of theosophy. Come here, you pretty butterfly!" she cried. "Sid is a greedy boy to keep you away so long. Go fetch the guitar; I am just in the humor for music."

Thus the woman countenanced the wooing, petting, and enriching with gifts the happy child, while she silenced my own doubts and those of the Doña Maria.

That Mrs. Sanderson was selfish, worldly, and at times mercenary, I well knew. However, these very attributes led me to believe that she would gratify herself and her son. I knew how thoroughly she would enjoy the absolute control of Mariposilla, how extravagantly she would equip her with the elegancies of life, exulting that Sidney's wife eclipsed always the beauty of other women.

Beauty she worshipped.

It had never occurred to her that Sidney might possibly marry a plain woman.

"If Sid should marry a homely girl, I should hate her," she said, one day. "Is he not splendid?" she would ask, when her son chanced to dwarf physically his associates.

And Sidney's exterior was admirable. He dressed perfectly, and there was about him the freshness of perpetual bathing. To Mariposilla he was the ideal type of masculine American elegance.

She scorned each day in her secret soul the careless, unconventional dress of the remaining Spanish men of her acquaintance, feasting her eyes with childish delight upon every detail of her lover's faultless attire.

Yet, withal, Sidney was not a fop. He was too blasé, and at times too sullen, to represent the gibbering class to which his immaculate and ultra-fashionable clothes might have otherwise attached him. But his unbounded reticence was his greatest protection; while it gave him, with some, a reputation for depth. Many believed that, although not brilliant in conversation, he sympathized silently with culture, and was shrewd in business affairs. In truth, Sidney had never taken an active part in his mother's financial transactions; but that her son was a dummy she carefully concealed. There was a laudable spirit in the woman's attitude. Her affectionate subserviency to her boy in the eyes of their friends was admirable.

I had so often seen wealthy mothers humiliate and belittle their sons, that, although I believed Mrs. Sanderson to be the business brains of the family, I was glad that she abstained from flaunting the fact.

I think I understood the elements of Mrs. Sanderson's character at that time quite well, with one exception. Unfortunately, I stopped too soon in my analysis. I innocently took it for granted that she possessed a moral side to her worldly and perhaps frivolous nature. Here was my fatal mistake. I did not understand that the woman would unflinchingly sacrifice any one for selfish, momentary enjoyment.

In all cases her own pleasure was suggested by the inclinations of her son. To keep him contented and passably respectable, she would have ruined her dearest friend.

Ethel Walton was arranging an entertainment to take place shortly after Easter. The girl was an enthusiast. Everything that she did called for her heart's best efforts.

Her present schemes were charitable. The Episcopal church needed an organ, and Ethel had determined that the necessary money should be raised. Her artistic and really poetic nature had found an outlet in the existing emergencies of her church, and she boldly originated a grand rose pageant. Each day she grew more enthusiastic over her prospects of success.

All the youth and beauty of Pasadena had been pressed into the carnival. The opera-house had been generously donated by the owner; while the papers each day keyed to the highest pitch the expectations of the public, by promising the most ravishing display of beauty and flowers ever gathered upon the celebrated Pacific Coast.

Even the Doña Maria had been beguiled into loaning treasures from the sacred green chest. But, best of all, she had generously consented to allow Mariposilla to dance, when Ethel explained, in her pretty way, that everyone was taking part, for the glory of Pasadena, if not for the church.

"Will you believe it?" she said; "I have had scarcely any opposition. My dances are all full, and I have two magnificent marches composed of beauties, whose scrupulous parents can't quite go the tripping, but are delighted to allow their consciences a constitutional walk."

The rehearsals were, of course, an interesting excuse to go to Pasadena; and each week we drove over with Mariposilla. At home she was continually practicing her steps, and the clicking of castanets soon grew familiar. She was alive with enthusiasm and expectation; while her costume to be worn upon the eventful night became a matter for our united thoughts, before it was at last satisfactorily designed.

It was all that the Doña Maria could do to restrain her restless child through the long, religious hours of Good Friday. When they knelt together in the old church, Mariposilla listened not to the solemn prayers. Sternly her mother rebuked her inattention; but the girl's eyes were flooded with happy dreams, and she forgot over and over again the crape-draped cross. The pictures of the stern, gloomy saints failed to frighten her into a state of contrition. Only to the Virgin did she sometimes lift her wandering eyes to implore protection for the lover now absent from her side.

When the sun rose gloriously upon the last day of the penitential season, Mariposilla's spirits rose too. Nothing could restrain her.

"I am most tired of prayers!" she cried, innocently joyous in her emancipation, as we went together, at the request of the Doña Maria, for lilies.

Like a field of snow in the sunshine the tall, pure flowers bloomed in symbolic beauty, for the world's glad festival. Our offering to the sweet Mother and the holy Child was a thousand—and on Easter day they would make glorious the old church.

For years the Doña Maria had dressed the ancient Mission for Easter, and for several seasons her daughter had also assisted. Now for the first time the girl plead excuses.

She wanted to go to Pasadena with Sidney and Mrs. Sanderson, as there was to be a rehearsal of her dance in the afternoon and Ethel had urged them to drive over early and lunch at Crown Hill.

Sadly the Doña Maria turned from the basket of white roses she had just gathered.

"What!" she exclaimed, "does my child refuse to honor the sweet Mother and the holy Child? Never before has she thought it other than joy to arrange the holy altar."

"Forgive Mariposilla, dear Doña Maria," I said. "Let me assist this year, and later, when the work is completed, I will drive the child myself to the rehearsal."

To this arrangement the mother agreed, and in consequence we had gone for the lilies early, reaching the old church in advance of other workers.

As we drove through the long, shaded roads of San Gabriel, the waysides seemed lined with devotees. Everyone was going to some church with flowers. Wagon-loads of lilies and roses were soon a common, though not less beautiful spectacle. Loveliest of all were the little children, hastening eagerly upon their sweet errand, with arms almost hidden beneath fragrant burdens.

We met one small child carrying in proud distinction a cross of violets. Another bore a crown of golden poppies, smiling with the light of the foothills.

When we approached the Mission, groups of Mexican children, many of them in their bare feet, thronged about us with funny little offerings, composed of flowers whose astonishing tones were often a mad blending of orange and deep pink.

The near advent of the happy festival had awakened in these humble breasts and uncultivated natures a God-given love for the beautiful. Each arrangement of flowers told a touching story. In every bunch was hidden the angel of the child who gathered it.

When we halted with our fresh burden, Father Ramirez, who was standing in the doorway of the ancient church, hastened with courtly consideration to assist us. The old priest commanded the staring children (in Spanish) to carry the flowers into the church, as he gallantly hitched our horse.

Once free from the wagon, I found it impossible to resist the picturesque old stone stairway, which leads from the ground to the choir above. Stealing a moment from my duties, I ran up the rough, time-worn steps, and from a little overhanging balcony caught the morning vision of the valley, stretching peacefully beyond.

"Some time I must come here in the moonlight," I said, as I descended and entered the chilly old church. "Surely I would learn sweet secrets which the sun each day effaces."

# XVIII

It had been an eventful day for Ethel Walton. Now but a brief half hour remained to determine the creditable success of the rose pageant.

With a sandwich in her hand, she had slipped into the rear passage leading to the door of Mrs. Sanderson's box.

"No, I can't come in," she replied to her friend's entreaty to enter. "I want just one little peep at the audience, while I eat my supper. I must feel particularly inspired in this last dreadful moment. And the house is grand," she exclaimed, triumphantly. "'Delightful to the ravished sense,'" she hummed, enveloping herself gleefully in the folds of a sheltering portière.

"What a relief, after all these weeks! Sister has just come from the front, where they are actually speculating on the tickets. It sounds too good to be true. I hear the distant strains of the new organ!" she cried, dramatically. "If only we can postpone the murder of the calcium light man by our bloodthirsty Professor Tiptoe success is ours!"

She flew gaily from the box to attend to the last few arrangements that prefaced the overture.

Pasadena's handsome opera house had been, possibly, the supremest blessing of the great boom. At the time it was built, few doubted the absolute necessity of a rival city for the south of the State. Fortunately for beautiful Pasadena, the men with visions were ruthlessly awakened to find Los Angeles still the acknowledged commercial center of the valley. In the meantime, her aristocratic suburb had an opera house and a number of other delightful conveniences that might have been delayed in the absence of a boom.

The audience assembled upon the night of the pageant indicated assured prosperity. The sight was an opulent surprise for the uninstructed stranger. Not a vacant seat was visible. The upper galleries were crowded to the wall; many were standing in the aisles.

From our box we rejoiced for Ethel in the finished brilliancy of the scene.

"Every one in the set is here but the Prince of Wales," Mrs. Sanderson remarked, jestingly, as she surveyed with honest astonishment the elaborate equipments of the evening.

Extending completely around the balcony, across the proscenium, and encircling both upper and lower boxes, bloomed a variegated band of exquisite roses, four feet in width.

MARY STEWART DAGGETT

Here and there the luxurious band turned from a knot of glorious Duchesse into a stretch of Maréchal Neil, which farther on caught hold of the vivid Henrietta. Touching close the pure French rose-color, the simple, unaffected La Marque lay like a field of snow between voluptuous meadows—for next beyond, almost throbbing, scintillating with every change of the lights, shone the Gold of Ophir.

In its distinctive beauty, it seemed to steal from the wonderful galaxy of bloom the composite glory of all.

Last in the wonderful band, the Jacqueminot imparted its dark beauty, also its rich odor of high-born culture that lingers in the petals long after their color has fled.

Although the general scheme of the pageant had been a secret, it was soon understood that the roses used in the decoration of the auditorium were sympathetic representatives of those personified upon the stage.

Each dance was to be an idealization of a particular rose. In the audience, personal preferences were quite noticeable; for favorite dances were boldly championed, not only in corsage bunch and boutonnières, but by superb bouquets of enormous size.

It is doubtful if more beautiful floral decorations were ever seen. Viewed from the stage, the dress circle and parquet appeared a huge garden of beauty; the boxes, fairy bowers, twined with their representative roses.

Those attending, almost without exception, were in full evening dress.

Gay parties of visitors from the various hotels waited eagerly for the rise of the curtain, satisfied that the decorations of the house justified great expectations for the performance. Anon, were heard surprised confessions from the provincial Easterner, who had for the first time discovered the existence of a civilized West.

Mrs. Wilbur laughingly owned that her only opportunity for enjoying a peep at the notorious "wild and woolly" was one afternoon when she had gone into Los Angeles to a wild and woolly show from New York. The show pretended to represent the common peculiarities of the West, whereas she blushed to acknowledge it an embarrassing portrayal of Eastern conceit and prejudices.

Mariposilla was to dance in the Spanish dance. She was to personify the Gold of Ophir rose—their subtle charms would mingle at last.

It is hardly necessary to relate that our box bloomed with her chosen rose; that we ourselves heralded our devotion by wearing no rose but the Gold of Ophir.

As the overture died away, the curtain lifted upon a scene at once familiar with local beauty. The time of year was supposed to be November; and at the foot of the protecting Sierra Madre, whose tops stretched away in the distance, we beheld the old garden of Las Flores. The gray haze of summer still hung about the peaks, for the Silver Harlequin, the son of the mighty Rain God, had not come.

Nature was inactive, as yet unable to overcome the lethargy of her annual rest.

In the garden, sheltered by interlacing trees and tall palms, upon a couch of verdure, slept the goddess Flora—her pagan spirit now at last purified and free, after weary wanderings in regions of ice and snow.

Close to the Goddess slumbered the golden Poppies, who ring always the first sweet bells of spring. The Poppies were dainty children, whose golden heads and gowns of yellow and green told instantly the story of the Foothills. The music, which from the first had been soft and dreamy, now suddenly grew harsh. Its poetry was gone, for stealing into the peaceful garden came the ashy Breath of the torrid Desert.

At last he had outwitted the Silver Harlequin, the son of the mighty Rain God! and his diabolical joy was horrible to behold. His agile movements were wonderful, as he appeared to actually float through the air. One moment he leered at the unconscious Goddess, the next he satirized, in a demoniac dance, the belated Harlequin. Then, unable to control his mad fury longer, he summoned from his desert kingdom an army of Cacti to despoil the beautiful Valley. At the head of this evil legion, bristling with cruel needles, and grotesquely formidable in its reality, the Breath of the Desert took formal possession of the Happy Valley. Through excited gestures he commanded the Cacti to take root in the fruitful land, to spear the charming plants and choke the tender flowers; while he breathed upon the sleeping Flora his own fiery breath, that she might never again gaze into the shining face of the Silver Harlequin, or feel the touch of the gentle maiden, Spring.

But his conquest is short, for, even as he exults, the Silver Harlequin appears, glittering and strong, from the realms of the Rain God.

In his hand is the magic sword with which he fells to the ground the now powerless Cacti; then, in majestic anger, challenges to single combat the vile usurper.

A moment the irreconcilable enemies pause, and then ensues a deadly fight; thrilling and uncertain as the passionate music leads it on. Again and again each combatant strives for mastery. Implacable hate flashes from their burning eyes as their merciless swords strike fiercer and fiercer. Now, wilder grows the combat; wilder speaks the music, until at last the fatal plunge is made. The magic sword of the Rain God's son has triumphed. At the feet of the glittering Harlequin the Breath of the Desert falls.

The music then sank into a low, sweet whisper of melody, while at the same instant the precious rain was heard. The veil of mist ascended from the glad "Mother Mountains," and a glorious rainbow proclaimed the advent of the gentle maiden, Spring, who came joyfully from the Magic Cañon. In her train danced a company of wee, fairy raindrops, who deluged the Valley gleefully with showers from their sparkling wands.

Spring held in her hand the magic fern, stolen from the queen of the highest waterfall of the Enchanted Cañon. With her glittering band she descended the mountain to do obeisance before the mighty Harlequin; then with the wonderful fern she awoke the golden Poppies and the sleeping Goddess.

In the second scene, Nature is fully aroused, and gracious Flora smiles again. The maiden, Spring, pulsing with joy, clad in a robe of palest green, adorned with sprays of maidenhair from the far, cool cañon, the breath of almond blossoms in her golden locks, dances before the Harlequin the dance of Spring. Gliding about the garden she tells her wonderful secret with poetic grace, falling at last upon her knees before her shining master, who commands her to bid the Poppies ring once more the glad, golden bells of Spring.

No words are spoken. All is action—poetry in motion, intensified by music.

As the drop fell on each of the scenes, the house grew stormy with applause, the air sweet with flying bouquets; while the audience turned one to another to exclaim at what they had seen, and to speculate upon what was yet to come.

The curtain now rose upon the carnival of the Foothills.

The season had advanced to the latter part of February, and from field and roadside trooped the wild flowers.

In a succession of charming dances and marches, children and young girls personified, in artistic and sympathetic costumes, the wealth of wild flowers which each year adorns the Southern California spring. First came the Poppies, ringing long chimes of golden bells to the music of their dainty yellow feet, while close to them marched, in bewildering phalanx, the delicate lavender Brodiæas. The Brodiæas were graceful maidens in æsthetic gowns, overlaid with the effective flowers that trailed from a belt, like green silk cords tipped with purple tassels. Their pilgrim hats were solid with purple bloom; their long pilgrim staves a marvel of loveliness, covered with ferns and nodding lavender flowers.

Next came the Wild Daisies—dear little girls in quaint, creamy gowns, sprinkled with yellow field flowers. On their heads, demure Dutch caps produced the impression of careworn Gretchens, as they sat upon three-legged daisy stools, knitting their stint of a daisy stocking. Last, from the Foothills came the Baby-Blue-Eyes—wee men in blue, trundling small wheelbarrows overflowing with starry blue flowers.

When each group of wild flowers had in turn completed the dance or march expressing its idealized part in the carnival, they together formed into a triumphant tableau as the curtain fell, stormed again with enthusiastic applause.

But the event of the evening was yet to come. The rose pageant was about to begin, and Mariposilla would soon dance.

Thus far there had been no delay in the performance, no uncertainty, no halt. We rejoiced momentarily for those who had worked so tirelessly.

The director of the orchestra, a German, intense and enthusiastic, had worked hand in hand with Ethel to interpret to the highest degree her poetic ideas. The little man's delight was visibly manifest as the performance proceeded. Not once did the music halt, not once did the intelligent leader fail to intensify the climax of the stage.

When the drop rose for the grand pageant of the season a hush was upon the house.

Then murmurs escaped from all.

"How superb" exclaimed Mrs. Sanderson, her handsome, critical face softening with pleasure.

It was now the season of Easter; the rapturous Valley was in its glory. High up in the mountains, in a wooded cañon, fringed with growing ferns, beneath a canopy of roses, we beheld the Goddess. The simple outlines of her classic robe defined her nobly. Her charming, gracious bearing was beyond expression, her serene beauty the theme of all.

Before her knelt the Silver Harlequin.

With dignity the smiling Flora commanded him to arise and produce the pageant of Roses, the glory of the year. Now, in obedience to the Harlequin's magic sword, the Spirit of Easter is felt in the land. Mission chimes smite suddenly the air. The music deepens into a grand march, while the bells strike time to its solemn measures. Then appears a wonderful procession moving slowly to the old church; for from the far-reaching ranchos of the Valley have assembled strong youths and sweet señoritas. The snowy robes of the neophytes are embellished with symbolic stoles of white roses; in their hands they carry long fronds from the date palm, that wave as they march to the victorious strains of the music. The girls follow, wonderfully beautiful in the ever-changing lights that intensify their pure robes, or color, with violet, and green, and amber, the long, floating veils fastened to crowns of white roses. Pure roses deck their throats and glistening arms, while in their hands they bear tall tapers in rose candlesticks. Like a beautiful vision they pass and repass, the waving palms and shining tapers telling a sweet story of youthful devotion to a poetic religion. Then the music deepens, the fickle lights intensify, and the old bells ring sadly and solemnly the chimes of a picturesque and dead past.

As the White Roses drifted away, the scene suddenly changed.

In a blaze of light and music, the Silver Harlequin now called before the Goddess an array of dainty color and grace. Stepping the faultless measures of a court quadrille came the ladies of the Duchesse Rose. Clad in Empire gowns of pink, garlanded with pink roses, wearing huge hats from under whose rose-laden brims they glanced with coquettish charm, they took all hearts by storm.

Next in the marvelous pageant came the Yellow Butterflies, born in the hearts of the great Maréchal Neil. One by one they flitted with bright yellow wings from the dark hiding-places of the garden.

The sixteen glancing creatures were blondes. Golden hair floated about their white shoulders, and golden crowns sustained the jeweled antennæ, which quivered while they danced. Maréchal Neil roses clung to their gowns and smiled into their faces, as they poised and wavered in the gorgeous, ever-changing lights.

Now from the distant Orient were seen approaching dark beauties clad in the purest rose color. They were borne by slaves of the Sultan in sumptuous sedans covered with rich Henrietta roses. As the beauties left their flower chairs, they posed gracefully before the goddess, then sped away to perform a charming tamborine dance, which fully realized the now exalted expectations of the audience.

Hardly had the roses of the Orient vanished before the garden was again brilliant. The sweet Jacqueminots had come in dainty aprons, big kerchiefs, and colonial caps. Industriously the pretty maidens plied the rose-twined spinning wheels of their grandmothers, until the imaginary stint was spun; then, abandoning their picturesque wheels, they joined in an old-fashioned dance upon the green.

When the colonial maids had passed from sight, followed by rounds of patriotic applause, Mrs. Sanderson moved nearer to the front of the box.

"The señoritas have discharged their spiritual duties; they are coming now to dance," she said, smiling, as she eagerly scanned the side approaches of the stage.

She had but ceased to speak when from secluded Spanish gardens, flourishing now only in the imagination of the aliens who destroyed them, came the dark, happy, historic señoritas.

Emotional, fickle, passionate—rare personifications of their typified rose—the matchless, wonderful Gold of Ophir. A hush of surprise for a moment pervaded the house; then its enthusiasm burst forth, when the sixteen señoritas began to weave and glance in the intricate measures of an old Spanish dance.

"Where," whispered Mrs. Wilbur, "did Miss Walton find these marvelous creatures? And how did she create such costumes?"

"The coloring is perfect," Mrs. Sanderson declared. "The fickle shading is all there, showing in every detail. See how the Ophir buds nestle in the yellow lace mantillas. The effect is thrilling."

Fast and daintily flew the thirty-two golden feet. Brilliantly flashed the jewels on the white arms, swung high at the bidding of castanets. Then the spirit of the music changed, and the señoritas vanished into the shadow of the trees, to return instantly with gorgeous hoops of Ophir roses. Dancing again, they formed at last on each side of the garden.

From this living phalanx of bloom, extending like twin sprays of the marvelous Ophir, sprang Mariposilla.

Shaming not her prototype, she stood before us, the vision of all that we had anticipated.

For a moment she hesitated, trembling like an Ophir bud in the breeze. Then her lovely, tearful eyes sought for Sidney. For once in his life, the man forgot himself. For once, honest emotion swayed him.

Leaning unconsciously from the box, enamored, forgetful of the audience, spellbound, he snatched from his coat the rose that Mariposilla had given him. Pressing it to his lips, he flung it at the feet of the trembling child.

It was enough. The dancer's response told passionately, without words, what she never could have said.

Her form seemed suddenly enveloped in translucent light. She was oblivious to everything but the rapturous moment.

Clad in the fatal satin skirt of the Doña Maria's little dead sister; about her throat, the coveted necklace of opals, and, draping her beautiful head, the filmy yellow wedding lace of her mother, she danced as she never danced before. She seemed a marvelous apparition, freed from a haunted chamber of the Alhambra. With every step, with every movement of the palpitating figure, with every droop of the deep-fringed eyelids and every fling of the glancing arms, the ecstatic passion of her young life was manifest.

Unconsciously she imparted to the dance of her nation the tragic possibilities of her nature.

Forgetting all restraint, all method, she abandoned her liberated body to the emotions of her throbbing soul.

Long afterward, all remembered how she had swayed the great house into irresistible tumult; then suddenly had floated mysteriously away, lost in the dazzling retreat of the señoritas.

The pageant terminated with a superb tableau, symbolizing the end of the prolific rose season.

At Easter, and for a number of weeks after, nature grows prodigal. Then comes a lull. The roses have exhausted themselves. The brilliant carnival is over, and a number of weeks must now elapse before the vines and bushes gather strength to flower again.

With an appropriate accordance to reality, the closing tableau represented, with poetic significance, the return of Spring, accompanied by wild flowers and roses, to the Magic Cañon.

From the front of the garden the brilliant procession wound upward in tiers of harmonious color, until, far above in the mountains, the Silver Harlequin and Spring stood close to the entrance of the Magic Cañon. From the heart of this enchanted spot all had issued—a divine secret; all were again returning to sleep until nature bid them once more arouse. This last magnificent spectacle was glorified by strong rose lights; while from above a silent rain of variegated rose petals fell like a soothing benediction.

When the curtain was at last down, the artistic and financial success of the pageant was the theme of the entire community.

The profits of the matinée, to be given the next afternoon, would more than defray expenses, and the proceeds of this victorious night would be safe.

Ethel and her able assistants were happy with excitement. Upon the now demoralized stage they were receiving congratulations from throngs of friends. Ethel stood like a delighted child between her father and the rector, when Mrs. Sanderson approached to utter the pretty things she always said so well.

At her side stood Mariposilla, flushed and submissive to the woman's bold caresses.

"Our little Butterfly is weary after her wonderful flight," the lady said, turning to the rector in her inimitable way. "Bring the little one's cloak, Sidney," she continued, addressing her son, who went at once to find a rich, fur-lined garment belonging to his mother.

"There," she said, when the young man returned with the wrap and placed it solicitously about Mariposilla, "the dear child will now be quite safe from a cold."

The running hither and thither was at last decreasing. The lights were growing dim and the performers were rapidly dispersing. We ourselves were just leaving the stage, when Ethel flew to my side and claimed Mariposilla for the night.

"She must come home with me," she declared. "I want to take care of her for to-morrow. It is perfect nonsense for her to drive to San Gabriel when she must return at noon to-morrow. I am determined to have my own way to-night," she cried. "It is the duty of all to spoil me this once," she declared, when Sidney interfered, volunteering to bring Mariposilla to the opera house in good season the next day.

"No, sir," said the girl with an oracular shake of her finger, "Mariposilla belongs to me to-night. You may control her movements after to-morrow."

Reluctantly the child yielded to the decision of Ethel. As she parted from her lover she unconsciously smiled up into his face a regretful good-night that answered touchingly his own silent renunciation.

# XIX

E thel went early to the opera house the morning after the eventful night of the pageant. The flowers would need freshening, and the girl was determined that the matinée should give full satisfaction to those who had been denied the excitement of the opening night. She knew that many delicate persons and children would attend in the afternoon. There would also be critical ones, who, having failed to secure tickets in time for the evening performance, would come to the matinée, perhaps with ungenerous spirits. For these reasons Ethel desired that the decorations of the house and stage should both delight and astonish, as they had done upon the previous evening.

Afterward the girl told how she had felt almost like weeping when she entered alone the dark, chilly opera house.

"It seemed like a great tomb, with its thousands of wilting roses," she said. "Until joined by others, I was filled with a horrible depression. I felt as if something miserable was about to happen. The flowers really looked no worse than I had expected, for the gorgeous band was still effective; but its first, perfect freshness was gone, its roses were dying, and I was alone at their death. Of course," she continued, "I felt better when we covered the withered places with fresh roses, but I was still restless and foolishly apprehensive."

Yet, with all the girl's uneasiness, she had little time for indulging nervous presentiments. There was much work to be done, and the time was short. Even when the decorations had been satisfactorily freshened, her unreliable performers would have to be looked after.

One girl had left a candlestick, which must be retrimmed; another had forgotten to take home her hoop, which had to be twined with fresh Gold of Ophir roses. Last of all she must collect and sort carefully all the necessary articles that would be called for by fair irresponsibles at the very last moment.

When I joined her in the green room at one o'clock, she looked anything but dejected, as she dabbed energetically the contents of a rouge pot onto the cheeks of a procession of maidens, filing in turn before her.

"There! go in peace, and dance your best," she cried, flinging away the ruddy rag as the last of the file passed on to the artist who was doing the eyes.

"Everything moves anxiously to-day," the girl said, pathetically, while she rested a moment against the wall. "I suppose I am a simpleton, but I feel as if the crack of doom were at hand. Mariposilla is late, although I told them to send her at half past twelve, and the Harlequin's wife has forgotten his cap," she said, almost hysterically, as she turned from my side to answer a volley of unnecessary questions.

"Where shall we go, Miss Walton?"

"Miss Walton, can't I have some paint on my cheeks?"

"Please, Miss Walton, my slipper is untied!"

"Miss Walton, my sister has lost her hat."

"Go directly onto the stage and stay, in readiness for your positions," the girl answered, distractedly.

"Come," I said, hoping to take her a moment out of herself, "Come with me into one of the flies; I have something to tell you."

"Dear me," she exclaimed, "what can have become of Mariposilla?"

"She is safe to-day," I answered, as we entered the fly. "She is safe to-day! But what will become of her to-morrow? The Sandersons have gone!"

"The Sandersons gone!" the girl repeated, in excitement. "Where have they gone?"

"They left to-day at noon for New York, to enable Sidney to marry, if possible, Gladys Carpenter. Her father has just died. With his death the daughter inherits three millions."

The words had but escaped my lips when a commotion in the adjoining fly betokened some catastrophe. In a second we had pushed through a crowd of frightened girls, to bend in horror over the prostrate form of Mariposilla.

"She is dead," cried Ethel. "She heard what we said and our words have killed her."

"Hush!" I whispered, "she has only fainted. Get water quickly."

Ethel flew at my bidding, while I unfastened the little bodice that but a moment before had heaved so lightly with the pulsations of a happy heart. Dear little Butterfly, I thought, how cruelly have your poor little wings been crushed!

Hot, indignant tears rained from my eyes, as I superstitiously unclasped the opal necklace, once worn by the beautiful, unfortunate Lola.

Ethel had now returned with the water, and the crowd, still pressing about us, was creating a panic.

"Stand back," I cried. "Don't you see you are taking every breath of the air?" As I spoke, the excited, curious, theatrical throng fell away.

Enveloped in her mother's wedding lace, that in the fall had shrouded her with prophetic significance, Mariposilla lay like one dead, unconscious of a miserable awakening. As I bent beside her I almost dreaded to see the heavy fringes lift from the beautiful eyes that I feared would never shine again with their old happy light.

"Dear child!" I whispered, as I applied the water, "what can we do to mend your poor little broken heart?"

While I yet spoke, the delicate eyelids began to quiver, and a little hand to tremble. A tired sigh and then a stifled sob burst from the lips.

"Darling, be brave, you have only fainted. I will take you home to the dear Doña Maria," I said, as naturally as I could.

Mariposilla lifted her great sorrowful eyes in mute entreaty; then two heavy tears rolled to her cheeks, imploring me to fulfill my promise. I knew that it was best to take her home while she wished it.

In her weakness she had not the strength to realize her sorrow. She seemed almost to have forgotten the occasion of her shock, for she closed her eyes at once, and submitted almost unconsciously to her transportation to the carriage. Tenderly we placed her on the very cushions from which she had sprung, but a few hours before, radiant and expectant.

Would she not see Sidney! The cruel night, and the long, uneventful forenoon were at last over. Now she could dance again for her lover. When it was all over, she would ride away with him in the gay trap. He would tell her once more how fondly he loved her. Tell her how beautiful she was—how much more beautiful than the cold, wise Gladys. Then she would go again to the dear, bright hotel for dinner. She would sit by Sidney. He would watch her every desire, and when dinner was ended they would go to the pretty sitting-room, where she would look fearlessly into the silver shrine; for never again would she be jealous and weep. No, no! not when her lover had sworn that he loved not the cold, beautiful Gladys; that he cared not for her riches or accomplishments. Then, after a while, all would go to the ball-room; Sidney would lead her to dance, and Mrs. Wilbur would be unhappy. But she—she, Mariposilla, would be joyful!

Poor, foolish little Butterfly, flitting eagerly from flower to flower, drinking, unconsciously, deadly poison with honey, how cruelly different from the sweet dreams of the morning would be the realities of the evening!

While she ran gaily from the carriage at noon, full of sweet, innocent visions, the ironic interpretation of her pitiful fate was even then decided. For, flying from rash promises, flying from the distractions of her beauty, flying from the tardy entreaties of conscience—Sidney Sanderson and his mother had gone.

With every intervening mile they were outstripping her ruined love, were nearing the selfish goal of the mother's ambitions; nearing the desolate Gladys, who, bowed with grief, and ignorant of all, would take, at the entreaty of her dead mother's friend, the reluctant lover who could never make her happy.

Poor Gladys! Poor Mariposilla!

Even before I allowed myself to acknowledge the perfidy of the woman with whom I had been so intimately associated, I began to understand her, when, early in the morning, a groom from the hotel brought me a note, asking me to drive over at once, as they were to leave that day at noon for the East.

"Duty compels us to go," Mrs. Sanderson wrote, shamelessly.

The word "duty" aroused at once my suspicions. I felt with a creeping certainty that Gladys Carpenter was the woman's prey. I believed that some unexpected turn of fortune had revived Mrs. Sanderson's ambitions.

I was sure that she had at one time relinquished all hope of obtaining the heiress for her son; but I felt on my way to the hotel a sudden presentiment that, on account of some unlooked-for occurrence, she was going to New York to revive her abandoned schemes.

I felt an uncomfortable stiffness as I entered the once familiar sitting-room, now in a state of wild disorder.

Mrs. Sanderson was on her knees, packing the last trunk. Upon the floor were piles of clothing and innumerable trifles, which she had torn from the wall.

"Dear child! How good of you to come!" she said, extending her hand with brazen determination. "It would have broken our hearts to have left without seeing you. And dear Mariposilla! and Pet Marjorie, and the good Doña Maria—how can we ever be reconciled to leave them?"

"Why is your departure compulsory?" I asked, coldly.

The woman perceived instantly that I understood her, but her control was perfect. Her will was diabolical, yet for a moment a gleam of anger darkened her eyes. Then she answered naturally:

"Dear Gladys has lost her father. She is perfectly crushed, and has wired us to come at once."

I stood like a stone, while she told again of the intimate relations that had always existed between the families.

"Gladys is just like my own child," she continued, turning away her face with the pretense of forcing a protruding Indian basket into the trunk. "We are so disappointed to miss the matinée," she said, with her face still in profile. "Sid begged to stay until to-morrow, just to see Mariposilla dance, but I persuaded him that it would be brutal to neglect Gladys one moment longer than the necessary time for our miserable journey."

Before I could reply she had crossed the room to her son, who was fumbling over a finished trunk.

"Don't touch the things in the tray," she cried, nervously. "I never saw such a boy. This morning he actually packed books on top of my best tea-gown."

I knew that the insolence of the woman had cowed me. She was sublime in her villainy.

I stood helplessly rooted to the spot which I had first selected upon entering the room. Too weak to stand unsupported, I leaned against the table. My perverse silence must have astonished the woman, but she talked on loquaciously, appearing not to notice my lack of interest.

How I despised her! How hard she looked to-day, when only the night before I had thought her charming and humane.

Doubtless she had slept but little since she left the box in the Pasadena opera house. In the strong morning light she looked old and strangely haggard. Dark circles defined more clearly the faint network of wrinkles beneath her eyes. Her whole countenance was drawn with the tension of her anxious night.

Her aristocratic nose seemed elongated with the avaricious thinness noticeable in grayhounds when the chase is at its height. Even the delicate, shapely hands appeared parched and old.

Never again would I think of the woman as beautiful.

I saw her now for the first time in her true, deplorable character. With but one object to accomplish, her masterful selfishness had taken possession of her soul. Closing tightly its chamber, she refused to hear the entreaties of the outraged voice that plead in vain. For

Mrs. Sanderson, retribution was the ghost of the cowardly; repentance, a science to be skillfully ignored.

I could endure my thoughts no longer.

"Good bye," I said, coldly, as I walked mechanically to the door.

As I spoke, the woman raised herself with decision from the floor. With outstretched hands she attempted a fraudulent embrace; but I anticipated the movement in time to escape.

"No, no!" I cried, in childish tremolo; "you must not touch me. I will not pretend that I am sorry that I will never see you again. I will never forget what you have done. Now I will go away, despising you, to the unhappy child whose life you have ruined for selfish amusement and the idle entertainment of your son!"

At last I had spoken, and at last she recoiled before me.

Without waiting to hear what she would attempt to say, I fled like Lot from the City of Destruction. But fatal curiosity I had not, and I cared not how the Sandersons writhed in the fire of my indignation.

My only desire was to get out of the house and never see them again.

As I left the hotel the groom in waiting advanced to drive me home.

"I will walk," I said curtly, spurning even this last attention from the woman I had left.

Later in Pasadena, when I heard the departing shriek of the Overland, with its echo flung fatefully back from the mountains as the train rounded a curve, I knew that the Sandersons had cut loose forever from the complications of their San Gabriel episode.

In justice to Sidney, I believe him to have been the better of two bad people. I believe that in his sensual selfishness he would willingly have resigned his mother's ambitions in regard to a marriage with Gladys Carpenter, glad to enjoy, for a time at least, the simple fascinations and marvelous beauty of Mariposilla.

The man was so perfectly carnal, so easily bored by the least intellectual superiority in a woman, that I believe he would have remained true to his own choice, had it not been for his mother's threats and positive command to marry, if possible, the three millions at hand.

I know that the thought of the classic, high-bred, sorrow-bowed Gladys must have been a cold shock, after his recent associations with Mariposilla. He must have remembered long how the Spanish girl adored him openly with all her young heart. Perhaps even as he went away the man held in cowardly reserve the possibilities of a refusal from the heiress.

I knew without being told that the conflict between the mother and son had been bitter. The mother had conquered, but Sidney had managed to write a parting note to his abandoned sweetheart, which the poor child unfortunately received. His slender promises only delayed her final despair, making it hopeless for those about her to arouse her pride or to graft in her trusting heart a proper disdain for the false lover.

I afterwards read his cowardly note, and saw clearly its import.

Now that Mrs. Sanderson had at last wearied of her infatuation, the proud, high-born Gladys, with her millions, would eclipse a dozen Spanish beauties. Soon she would laugh and jest over the affair with her New York friends, describing Mariposilla delightfully, while she enlarged upon the poor child's passion for her son.

I have since wondered if the Spanish girl would have been happy had Fate consented to her choice. I sometimes believe that eventually the restraints and requirements of the untried life would have wearied her. I also believe that with a nature so true, so simple and affectionate, she would have done her best to excel in the eyes of those she loved. In a responsive atmosphere her proud ambition would have fulfilled her will. With the cold and critical she would have lost her subtle charm. Away from her mountains and unconventional life she might have learned sad lessons. She could never have conned them alone without an aching heart; for, like her rose, she would have grown pale and dejected away from the sunlight of love.

# XX

In Southern California that part of the year extending from the middle of November to the middle of May virtually represents to the stranger its season.

The secret of the delightful summer, tempered, especially in the San Gabriel Valley and the vicinity of Santa Barbara, by unfailing sea-breezes, would astonish the infidel tourist who has flown excitedly away, stubbornly denouncing the summer as unbearable. Perhaps he has experienced two or three warm days in May that have played a trick on the tardy trade winds. If so, he comprehends perfectly, from a few weeks' sojourn, the imminent danger of climatic cremation.

He believes, ignorantly, that he has fled from the mid tropics, when he mops the damp perspiration from his gigantic brain-front in the dizzy June of an interior town. Devoutly thanking the kind Providence that has returned him to Tuckersville, he proceeds to write for the Tuckersville *Sun* full particulars relating to the climate and limited resources of Southern California.

Still, contrary to the slanders of the Tuckersville man, the weather, with the exception of a few warm days in the early spring, remains delightfully cool from the middle of April until the middle of August.

September is possibly less agreeable, for it is then that people are apt to believe themselves tired or warm, and there is a general wishing for change.

In the sweet, quiet summer, one wishes for nothing.

Refreshing breezes from the broad Pacific extend inland for many miles, and if occasional warm days come, the coast is near by, always inviting for a day those who do not care to stay long by the sea, or cannot afford a protracted outing.

For those who desire weeks of recreation and salt bathing, the Pacific coast offers every advantage. On the irresistible Santa Catalina Island, at the pleasant hotels that dot the coast, or in the poor man's sequestered cañon close to the sea, there are opportunities of rest and enjoyment for all.

To the resident of the San Gabriel Valley, who truly loves its grand, natural beauty enough to enjoy the free gifts of each day, there is about the summer a never-ending sense of peace and rest.

The winter months are restless and rushing—full of social excitement and alive with indefatigable sight-seers. As long as the tourist is abroad in the land his presence is a perpetual challenge. His disappointments are personally felt each day by his friends.

It is unfortunate that much of the picturesque hospitality of earlier days should have given way to a more laborious and less charming mode of entertaining. Now, the Marthas of pretentious country houses and elegant villas are "cumbered about much serving."

I had fortunately escaped both convention and routine in my life with the Doña Maria Del Valle, but I had been drawn by degrees into an experience that, from the beginning, was an anxious strain. I was now almost ill; I needed a change and the sea.

Yet I dared not desert Mariposilla, for I felt daily the burden of the part I had taken in establishing her intimacy with the Sandersons. I was determined to restore, if possible, her stolen happiness. The child seemed now comparatively docile and less changed than I had feared. I did not expect her to resist at once her first crushing disappointment, but in a few weeks I expected to take her to the seashore, when I hoped to surround her with new friends and new pleasures.

Time alone could help her, and I was full of hope.

I had now fully determined to educate Mariposilla, to fit her, with the Doña Maria's permission, for intimate contact with the dangerous world.

So infatuated I became with my plans that I again misunderstood the girl, while I foolishly lost sight of her race inheritances.

I thought she would revive, after a time, as an American girl would have revived. I expected her to be restored, with new beauties of mind and character.

As the days went by and nothing unusual happened, I told myself, joyfully, that experience was working the cure. I believed that soon a womanly scorn would heal effectually the wound which Sidney Sanderson had inflicted.

The girl had not grown less beautiful. With her trouble there had come into her face, after the first wild paroxysms of grief, a look that I could not interpret. I know now that it was the reflection of hope, a hungry, superstitious expectancy that tugged hourly at her heart.

Sidney's parting note had inspired in the ignorant girl the faith that he would return.

She had grown very gentle. She went regularly to mass, and arranged flowers each day in front of the little Spanish Virgin. One day I noticed that she had wreathed the picture in ivy, and ever after the grotesque little Mother displayed her finery subdued by the dark, cool leaves.

In the child's own room was carefully treasured every trifling relic of Sidney's past devotion. She had decked the whitewashed walls, in imitation of Ethel Walton's æsthetic chamber, with every small, sweet souvenir of the winter. The favors she had received at the eventful holiday cotillion surrounded the little looking-glass. Above her bed hung a cane and a cast-off tennis cap of Sidney's; while tenderly hidden from sight, except when she opened the drawer each day to weep, were the innumerable trinkets and gifts that her false lover had given her.

Every empty candy-box and every withered flower had been lovingly saved.

She still wore about her throat the little necklace, but the bracelet she concealed pitifully beneath her sleeve.

Each day she dressed with unusual care, expecting always the return of her lover.

One day a lover came. Not Sidney, for whom her poor heart pined, but Arturo, her kinsman.

There was no scene, as we had feared, for the Doña Maria had warned the young man to restrain, for the present, all signs of impatient passion.

"Speak to her not of love," she said, sadly, when she had confided to the burning, indignant youth by her side the present state of Mariposilla's feelings. "The poor, foolish child yet believes that the American will return," she explained. "Be patient, dear son," the Doña Maria besought when Arturo chafed under his tedious restraint; "the American will soon marry the choice of his mother; then will my poor deluded child lie crushed; yet, by the will of God, she will revive.

"Tell her not yet of love, only of the success and riches which you have gained. Treat her gently, as a sister, and in time all may be as we desire."

It was surprising how considerate the handsome, hot-headed Arturo remained, restrained always by the quiet persuasions of the firm, quiet Doña Maria.

The boy's unexpected return had been full of comfort to the lonely Spanish woman. She loved her grandnephew as a son; while she rejoiced daily that the young man was growing more and more like her own lost Arturo, whose name he bore.

As the summer wore away, the Doña Maria grew content. She

believed that Mariposilla would outgrow her sorrow, that in time Arturo would be successful in his suit, and that she might yet live to hold in her arms the children of her dear ones—dark, rich little beauties, who would preserve through yet another generation the inheritance of the Spanish blood.

"How often did I weep when I thought of my child united not with one of her own race. When I saw in my dreams grandchildren—pale little ones that I could not love, I cared scarcely to live," she said, pathetically.

With the exception of the Doña Maria's mother, who was now confined to her bed, our household moved as usual.

Arturo took a masterful charge of the neglected ranch, and, as the summer advanced, a gradual calm pervaded both the land and the family.

Through the middle of the day all enjoyed the refreshing siesta, and by the early afternoon the ocean breeze was stirring delightfully. Great baskets of luscious fruits were picked daily and placed about the veranda. In the grape arbor a table held always a pitcher of cool lemonade, delightfully softened with fruit flavorings.

The Doña Maria loved to prepare pleasant drinks, and, now that Arturo had returned and Father Ramirez came more often to the ranch, the good woman had frequent opportunities for serving her friends.

She revived the pleasant Spanish custom of gathering in the arbor for light refreshments. Each day she grew happier and more hopeful in regard to the future of her child.

The old priest also believed that Mariposilla would soon recover from her childish disappointment and be but too willing to accept for a husband the handsome Arturo, who had now a half interest in a large quicksilver mine in Old Mexico.

During the quiet afternoons Arturo took the greatest pains to explain to Father Ramirez his plans and ambitions. In the old summer house the young man would spread out the map of Mexico, tracing eagerly the new railroads, while he located, enthusiastically, his mine.

"There is no country like it," the younger man would declare, joyfully. "I am impatient every moment that I remain away.

"Of course, the American hounds are stealing in, just as they stole into California. Their cursed gold ought to buy them Paradise; yet, in Mexico they can never be the aristocracy. The gates and doors of the old families will always remain barred to the pale thieves who seek to enter."

"Be not so angry with the strangers, my son," replied the old priest. "Remember that gold and brains are both necessary in the development of any undeveloped country. The Americans have both. Love of race is noble, but often it dwarfs the mind. The cosmopolitan will ever succeed, while the narrow and revengeful will generally fail. But here comes the Doña Maria, we will contend no more," the old priest exclaimed, joyfully, as he clasped the hand of his dear old friend.

"Arturo is a true son of Spain," he said, gazing into the burning face of the youth he had always loved. "He is unlike his generation. He should have lived earlier."

I had heard without attempting to listen. Through my open window I often caught snatches of conversation that gave me a pleasant insight into the lives of these most interesting people. The warm, unrestrained affection and tender social relations existing between the old priest and his parishioners were things that I had not until now understood.

I often heard, in quiet, half undertone, the name of Mariposilla. Sometimes Arturo grew passionate in spite of his discretion. Then the old priest would reprove him gently; for he was a born Jesuit, restraining all those about him with calm determination.

"Peace, my son, always peace!" he would say. "Time alone can do for us what haste could never accomplish. Soon the blow will descend, for the false lover will marry the heiress. The poor little one will be crushed for a time, and then she will revive.

"Remember, through these hard weeks of waiting, only your love. Let not anger or revenge fill your young heart. Keep that ever clean and pure, ready for the treasure it shall some day hold."

"I will try to obey, Father," the young man replied, rebelliously. "It is easy for you to reprove," he exclaimed. "You who have never known the misery of a hopeless love."

A strange shadow flitted across the old priest's face. "How knowest thou, my son, that I never battled with unrequited affection? Judge not that the old father is stone. He was once even as thyself. But God forbid that he should think of aught now but the world beyond, and poor souls trying to find it."

"Forgive me, Father," the young man said, tenderly. "I will be a good son, and, in return for my obedience, you shall one day order the chimes of Old San Gabriel to ring for my wedding."

# XXI

The announcement of the marriage of Sidney Sanderson to Gladys Carpenter reached us during the latter part of June.

We were indebted to Mrs. Wilbur for the New York papers in which we read the embellished details of the "strictly private nuptials." The several accounts agreed in pronouncing the marriage the most noteworthy matrimonial event of the early summer. The facts, in brief, were as follows:

"The beautiful bride, heiress to three millions, although in deep mourning for her father, had laid aside, only for the wedding ceremony, the somber robes of her recent bereavement. At the close of the impressive yet simple service, she had resumed her mourning, preparatory to the departure for Scotland. On the historic isle, sequestered in a romantic castle overlooking Loch Lomond, Mr. and Mrs. Sanderson would spend their honeymoon. Society had unanimously agreed that a match more suitable in every way had seldom occurred. The high social position of both parties, the beauty and fortune of the bride, combined with the popular traits of the handsome groom, pointed unmistakably to social leadership.

"The palatial home of the late Rufus Carpenter would, doubtless, become a recognized center, when his beautiful daughter again rejoined with her chosen husband, the charmed circle of the Three Hundred."

This is the substance of what we knew. All that we would ever certainly know of the two lives in question.

For us the history of Sidney Sanderson was virtually closed. I alone claimed the privilege of imagining his uneventful end.

A creditable career he could never have. A life of indolent luxury, environed by the ordinary excitements of club life, would be the probable limit of his achievements.

His domestic life would, in time, become a monotonous restraint.

In dismissing him, I will always believe that he thought often during the years of his aimless existence of Mariposilla. Her beautiful dark eyes, flooded with adoring love, must have haunted many of the indifferent hours spent with his highly refined, philosophical wife.

After the first cool understanding, when both the man and the woman acknowledged the disappointment that each felt in the other, their lives would run on quietly and indifferently, each moved by separate interests that enormous wealth made possible.

Their elegant home I can readily picture. Artistic rooms, undisturbed by little meddlers. Silent halls, in which echoed no voices of children.

Dark shades, often drawn close before the windows of a mansion deserted for months at a time, by reason of the protracted absence of both mistress and master, who seldom traveled in the same direction, finding, as the years made plainer the remoteness of their tastes and principles, that antipodal distances alone could insure for each a comparative comfort.

I learned from authority that Mrs. Sanderson escaped old age.

On the verge of the dreaded boundaries of infirmity her selfish energies gave way. An unexpected puff of disappointment chilled her nerve, while it extinguished, midway in its socket, the brilliant candle that had cheered no lonely heart, had illuminated no sorrowing soul.

For Mariposilla alone the announcement of Sidney's marriage contained crushing evidences of his final desertion. The poor child had always believed that her lover would return. We had never been able to convince her of the hopelessness of the dream.

Now that the blow had at last descended, we hoped for much.

Through all the long weeks we had done nothing but wait. Even now we must wait still longer. We dared not show impatience at the child's terrible grief, when she remained as one stunned, refusing, day after day, our sympathy and society.

It was only in the cool of the evening that she left her room to join the family upon the veranda. Then she would slip away by herself, hiding in the darkest corner among the vines, a listless shadow in white that we dared neither to comfort nor to rebuke.

The summer was now at its height; the days were warmer and the cool nights more welcome. The haze had thickened about the mountains; the sky was often without a cloud.

The seaside resorts were crowded with pleasure-seekers. Only the industrious ones of the Valley remained at home to attend to the immense fruit crops, ripening every hour.

The hotels and villas were undergoing repairs for the ensuing winter. Society, in a body, appeared to be rusticating at Santa Catalina.

We, too, would have gone to the sea, but sorrow held us down with a relentless grip. The once happy household of the Doña Maria Del Valle was no longer the abode of peace and joy.

Each day Mariposilla required more care, for she was now really ill. She went about the house and garden as usual, but we had thus far failed to arouse her from her grief. Each day she grew more silent and suspicious, shedding fewer tears, but refusing always to listen to a word of reproach against the man who had deceived her.

Now, in addition to the anxiety for her miserable child, another stroke had fallen upon the Doña Maria.

The angel of death had entered again her home—her aged mother was dying. Father Ramirez had administered the Holy Sacrament, and now only the most powerful opiates could relieve, temporarily, the aged sufferer, sinking away from a horrible disease that for years had been unsuspected.

To myself fell the incessant care of Mariposilla.

It was seldom now that the sad-eyed Doña Maria left her mother's chamber. She had procured a Mexican woman to superintend the household, while she devoted herself, lovingly and unceasingly, to the care of the sufferer. Day and night she watched alone, until I feared she would drop under the strain.

It was astonishing how tenaciously the aged woman lingered. Sometimes she would revive, with almost supernatural strength. Stimulated by the opiates, she would protest desperately against remaining in bed. The poor old creature seemed to think that the bed alone was responsible for her death.

In her less painful moments, when the opiates soothed without stupefying, she talked excitedly in Spanish, living always far back in the days of her prosperity.

She was again on the far-reaching rancho, riding by the side of her husband, or dispensing free hospitality to a house full of guests. Always with her were the two little daughters, Maria and Lola.

"She remembers not the sorrows which have befallen us," the Doña Maria would say with tearful eyes, that each day grew larger as the rings of sorrow deepened beneath them. "She mercifully believes that my dear sister and I are still little ones at home.

"We are continually running from her side with messages for the maids.

"Sometimes she commanded us to stop our play and go to the old church for prayers. Again, she coaxes our father to buy more jewels, that we may outshine in beauty our neighbors at the grand wedding, soon to occur upon a distant rancho, where there will be for days feasting and great joy.

"Is it not kind, dear Señora, that the old mother should depart among pleasant memories, knowing not of my poor child's humiliation?"

As the Doña Maria spoke, the glory of unselfishness lit for a moment with saintly beauty her dark, worn face.

"Yes, dear friend," I replied, "it is kind and sweet that the loved one can go to rest in peace, but it is wrong for you to refuse relief from the heavy strain of the sick-chamber. Oblige me this once by allowing your place to be filled. You will be ill, I am sure, if you take neither air nor rest."

"Thanks, dear Señora," she replied, "I am happy for your thoughtful care; but I can now no longer take rest away from my mother. Sometimes I fall, for a few moments, asleep by her side, but I wish always to be near, that I may watch tenderly until her spirit has flown.

"I should grieve sorely if another closed forever the dear eyes."

I saw that the devoted daughter was happiest performing alone the last few duties that after death grow measurelessly sweet, and said no more. A few hours later the Doña Maria stood at my door quiet and tearless.

"Dear Señora," she said, "my mother is dead."

"What can I do?" I cried, daring not yet to presume with sympathy. Under the first cold shock of the impalpable mystery, I longed for a task that would check the dreadful, unsatisfied questions that thronged my mind.

"There is little to do. Arturo had gone for Father Ramirez.

"If only the Señora will speak to my unhappy child, I shall be most thankful. Tell her that her grandmother is no more, but restrain her from coming for a time into the chamber of death.

"Soon I shall have done all. I shall then come for my child and lead her to the dear one."

As the Doña Maria finished speaking, she vanished from my side.

As I heard her close the door of her mother's room, I knew that she would first pray before the shrine of the little Virgin.

For a moment I listened in the silence, almost longing myself to entreat comfort of the image.

I remembered how I had fainted Christmas morning, and how gladly I had regained consciousness in the protecting presence of the little Mother. I knew that the Doña Maria would gain strength and courage before the shrine of her implicit faith, and my own heart hungered for a touch of palpable comfort.

What if the little image was only painted wood? It whispered something to the simple, aching heart that a stern theology could never say.

Alas! I knew that for myself there was nothing but blind hope and fruitless speculation. I could never have knelt before a picture or a shrine, but I envied, none the less, the Spanish woman who found peace and comfort, while I so often suffered in the dark, unsatisfied and rebellious.

When at last I heard quiet steps, I knew that the Doña Maria had arisen from her prayers. I knew that in her sorrowing heart there was a blessed faith, childlike and strong, that would help her to perform, quietly and correctly, the last sad offices for her dead.

# XXII

I sought in vain about the house and garden for Mariposilla.

The child had not been away from the ranch since the news of Sidney's marriage, and her sudden absence alarmed me.

I remembered that it was Saturday. Perhaps Mariposilla had gone to the old church for confession. Arturo had the pony, and for a moment I was in despair.

Fortunately a neighbor arrived with a horse and buggy, which I borrowed.

I was determined not to alarm the Doña Maria, and drove away at once in the direction of the Old Mission. The road, for the first time, seemed long and uninteresting. The neighbor's horse was an ancient nag, who discovered at once my impatience and inexperience. He absolutely refused to accelerate his midsummer dog-trot. The persuasions of a stranger he ignored.

Despairing, I submitted, while I vaguely questioned myself as to what I should do, in case Mariposilla had not gone to the church.

When at last I caught sight of the long, gray outline, hiding among cool, green peppers, my heart seemed to stand still.

As I turned into the main approach leading to the Mission, the old bells broke suddenly the oppressive silence. Their melancholy strokes were for the dead; perhaps for the Doña Maria's mother, I thought.

Mechanically I counted the tolls, until their number had reached sixteen, then the old bells paused a moment before they again repeated the years of the youthful dead.

Upon approaching nearer I perceived that a funeral procession had just left the church. An assistant priest and a barefooted Mexican altar-boy stood framed in the arch of the ancient portal.

The sad little procession was now entering the old graveyard at the rear of the Mission. I could hear the sobs of the mourners, and my heart went out to the poor mother, garbed in faded mourning, bowed with both grief and labor.

The little coffin was borne on a bier by six swarthy young Mexicans, possibly one of them the lover of the dead girl.

The sight was pathetic, and at this particular time I felt it to be more than I could bear.

A moment later I peered into the old church—it was empty.

Where now could I go? To whom should I apply for help?

Father Ramirez was evidently not about; a strange priest had followed the funeral procession, and doubtless the old friend of the Del Valles had gone at once with Arturo.

I had probably missed passing them by taking a different road, having endeavored to shorten the distance by a cut through a ranch.

Mechanically I climbed into the buggy, believing that there was no course left but to return home for assistance, when in the distance I saw, almost like a sign from on high, the deserted hotel of East San Gabriel.

Without stopping to consider the probable absurdity of my surmise, I started the old horse upon the maddest race of his life.

In my excitement the wielding of the whip was a nervous joy.

The old bones of the beast seemed almost to crack as he leaped along the road.

All at once I seemed to be acting without reason, for when I at last entered the grounds of the deserted caravansary, there were no evidences to justify my suspicions.

The summer's silence was intense; not a human being was visible, and the desolation pervading the deserted resort was sickening as well as satisfying.

I felt that I had been absurd to believe for a moment that Mariposilla could have wished to reënter the place, and I was also convinced that, in her feeble condition, she could never have walked the distance from the ranch.

The old horse was now resting in front of the silent hotel, and my very inaction was unbearable. I racked my brain to the verge of despair, before I again hit upon a possible explanation for Mariposilla's disappearance.

Why had I not thought of it before? Why had I taken it for granted that Arturo had gone alone for Father Ramirez? The priest drove always in his own conveyance, and what could be more natural than to believe that Arturo had induced Mariposilla to accompany him upon his errand? Was it not reasonable to believe that the young people had laid aside their personal feelings at such a time, desiring to perform together a last, trifling duty to the dead grandmother?

True to the comforting inspiration, I had turned the reluctant horse to leave the grounds, when, rushing joyfully in front of the astonished brute, I beheld the hounds, Mariposilla's grayhounds, who knew where their little mistress was hiding.

Hastily hitching the horse to the nearest tree I reconnoitered at once the long veranda. Each door that I tried was locked; the windows were fastened, and the inside blinds closed.

Close at my heels followed the dogs, now wildly excited.

As a last resort, I decided to urge them to lead me.

"Dear Pachita! dear Pancho!" I cried, patting encouragingly their long, beautiful heads, while I entreated their almost human eyes to reply. "Take me to Mariposilla."

"Where is Mariposilla?" I repeated, slowly, "your dear little mistress, Mariposilla?"

For a moment, the poor brutes whined piteously; the next, they had darted away to the rear of the hotel.

I followed hotly, and at the corner of the house I perceived them wild with excitement at the foot of the escape ladder, leading from the ground to the upper veranda.

I needed no more to convince me of the truth.

Mariposilla had ascended the ladder which the dogs had not been able to scale. The half-frantic girl had sought to enter again the rooms once occupied by the Sandersons.

I delayed no longer. In a moment I was above, trying in vain the doors. As I approached the window of Sidney's now deserted bedroom, I perceived instantly that its glass had been shattered, and knew at once that Mariposilla was within.

For a moment, I stood rooted with apprehension; I dared not enter. A horrible dread deprived me of strength, until from within a piteous sobbing, more musical, more welcome than any sounds which I had ever before heard, told me that the child I sought was safe.

"Thank God!" I cried, springing into the room.

There, upon Sidney's deserted bed, upon his pillow, lay Mariposilla.

For a moment I shrank away, for the child had not heard me enter. I would willingly have allowed her the full extent of her strange, unusual consolation. Now that she was safe, I would have stayed with her the remainder of the afternoon, but the thought of the Doña Maria compelled me to speak.

"Dear child," I said, approaching the bed; "you must come home. We are in great distress. Your grandmother has just died."

"Just died?" she repeated, touchingly. "Why can I, too, not die? Indeed, kind Señora, I am most tired of life; I would gladly go with my grandmother."

"No, dear," I answered, "you must not want to die. It is wrong for you to remain so miserable. You should remember your dear mother, and try to recover your spirits, to be once more our good, happy child.

"Think no more of Sidney; dismiss now forever from your thoughts the selfish man who has deceived you."

Like a young tigress wounded into fury, the girl sprang from the bed.

"I blame him not," she cried, passionately. "It is the wicked, wicked Gladys who has stolen his love. I knew she would coax him from me when she sent so often her beautiful face to his mother.

"She loved him much, I was sure, but he said always that he loved her not in return; that she made him most tired, when he must listen to her learning and long words.

"That he loved none but me—poor, little Mariposilla, who knew nothing but to love him only."

"Yes, dear," I said; "you have loved as few ever love. I pity the man who has thrown lightly away your warm, true heart; but I know that after a time you will cease to pine. You will see that Sidney gave you up, not because Miss Carpenter was more beautiful, or that he loved her more, but because she had millions of dollars to make his life luxurious and idle.

"Be a brave girl," I continued, noticing with pleasure that the child had brightened visibly at my words. "Be good and brave for your own sake, and for the sake of the dear Doña Maria.

"Come home before you are missed, or your mother will be greatly distressed by your absence."

Obediently she followed me from the room, and down the ladder. As we drove away from the grounds she threw her arms about my neck and sobbed pitifully.

"Dear, kind Señora," she cried, "I will be good; indeed I will be good.

"If Sidney loves Gladys only for gold, he will yet come back! he will yet be mine!"

It was impossible for me to misunderstand the girl's passionate meaning. I trembled at the recollection of the opportunities and temptations of the winter. For the first time a terrible realization of the child's Spanish inheritances seized me. I felt that she would never acknowledge moral barriers to be a final restraint to her denied destiny; never be able to resist the undisciplined desires of her heart.

For the present I could not hope to unfold the immoral, or impossible consequences of Sidney Sanderson's return. Nothing but time and angelic patience would enable me to make plain to the ignorant girl the arbitrary laws of fate.

# XXIII

The sun had departed for the day, the evening had flushed and died in the cool arms of night.

In the chamber of death there was now the breathless calm which follows when all has been done.

Before the little Virgin, and about the spotless bed, where in purest linen slept the mother of the Doña Maria, holy candles had been lighted. Still unmolested stood the small stand covered with a fine drawn linen cover, upon which had rested for weeks the tumblers and bottles needed now no longer.

"See," the Doña Maria said tenderly, "see the spoon in the potion I had prepared but a moment before the poor suffering body found peace."

When I offered to remove the medicines, the devoted daughter was not willing.

"Touch not the table yet, kind Señora," she pleaded. "Wait until the dear body has been taken away; then will I find courage to disturb the tumblers that the dear hands once held."

As the Doña Maria spoke, Mariposilla entered the room, bearing a little cross of white roses. She laid it timidly upon the breast of her grandmother; then, frightened and hysterical, she fled from the bed.

"Poor child," said the Doña Maria, "she fears death greatly. She thinks only of the fire that must at first purify the soul, not of the joys of eternity.

"Go now, Señora, retire at once for the night. You are weary and in need of rest.

"I care not for company. I will remain alone with my mother and our blessed Lady. I desire to entreat that the sufferings of the dear one may be short.

"Surely the dear Lord will have mercy upon the aged one who has already endured so much upon earth."

"Good Doña Maria," I plead, "you will surely be ill if you kneel all night in prayer. To-morrow will be a sad, hard day, and without rest you will be unfit for its strain."

"No, Señora," she replied firmly; "I shall not be ill. After midnight I shall sleep; until then I shall pray."

I saw that my persuasions were in vain, and left her alone with her dead.

As I passed through the living-room to reach my own, I was startled by a white-robed figure in front of the Virgin's picture.

The full July moon, streaming through the open door, discovered touchingly the hopeless misery of Mariposilla. She was in her nightgown, gazing piteously into the illuminated face of the unsympathetic doll above the chimney shelf.

As I approached her, she turned sadly from the picture.

In the moonlight, I saw great tears shining in her eyes.

"She loves me not; she is angry and smiles no more," she said, despairingly.

The child's lovely face expressed so perfectly the agony of desertion that I felt powerless to comfort her. Her firm belief in the Virgin's displeasure had torn from her heart its last hope. For weeks she believed that the little mother would have mercy, would intercede for her, and restore in some miraculous way her lover; but to-night the Virgin would not smile. She refused to pity her sorrowful child.

"Dear Mariposilla," I said, remembering the tactics that I sometimes employed with Marjorie; "you must not think because the Virgin refuses to smile that she is angry.

"We ourselves cannot smile. We are sad and awed by the presence of death, and surely it would be heartless for 'our Lady' to smile, when those who love and trust her are in trouble.

"You are nervous and weary. You shall room with me to-night. I have already prepared you a nice bed upon my couch."

I drew her gently in the direction of my room, persuaded that I had quieted for a time her moody fears.

"No! no!" she cried, bursting away from me; "I can not sleep. I will never sleep again."

She rushed, passionately, through the open door into the moonlight. In her bare feet, clad only in her flowing nightgown, she stood like a spirit among the dark vines and lacy shadows of the old veranda.

Her hair fell about her shoulders like a tragic veil, while a sudden agony touched her young, white face.

"You know not what I have suffered," she sobbed. "You think I shall forget, but I never shall. I can not bear that he should not be mine."

"If only he had gone away like my grandmother, I could endure never to see him again. He would then be mine! all mine, and I could go joyfully into a convent and pray always for his soul."

Her voice had grown tearless and sharp.

From the corner of the house a tall, dark form was approaching.

"Come in quickly," I whispered; "Arturo is listening."

She obeyed me now, sinking wearily, as we entered my room, upon the waiting couch.

I was devoutly thankful when I believed her to be sleeping.

She had scarcely stirred for nearly an hour, and I told myself, wearily, that I, too, might perhaps catch a little rest. The day had been a perpetual strain. I was not expecting or intending to sleep soundly, but I felt a merciful relief in lying quietly by the side of Marjorie.

For the night, at least, Mariposilla was safe. I could only hope that the morrow would dawn more tranquilly than the trying day now, at last, over.

After the funeral, I intended to go immediately to Catalina with Marjorie and Mariposilla. I would wait no longer; the heartbroken child must leave San Gabriel at once.

I was arranging my plans most carefully, when I fell asleep from absolute exhaustion.

When I awoke, the moon was no longer casting fantastic shadows. My white walls were no longer softened by elfin touches.

The shadow vines and pepper branches had disappeared in the honest light of the July sun.

The morning was yet deliciously cool, but the day was fairly begun, even now brimful of sweet odors and bird-music.

The mockers, who had sung all night, were not yet weary, but less belligerent. At night they sometimes quarreled, but in the morning their little disagreements were adjusted.

As I delayed to open my eyes, half awake, but unwilling to shock too soon the last lingering desire to doze, I seemed to hear a familiar rebuke from the great pepper tree beyond my window.

"Señora! Señora! Señora!" called an old mocker. "Get up! get up! get up!" screamed his neighbor from the next limb.

I fancied now as I listened, that the birds had tried to awaken me in the night. Vaguely returned an ugly dream, with the ceaseless call of the persistent birds.

In a moment I remembered all. The dead grandmother, Mariposilla, the midnight cry of the mockers—"Señora! Señora! Señora!"

Mariposilla?

Where was she? When had she slipped away? Did the birds alone know?

The couch was empty. Each pillow bore the mark of the child's weary head.

In the night, while I slept, my restless captive had fled.

I sprang across the hall to her room; it was empty, and the bed undisturbed. Trembling I entered the death chamber. The Doña Maria was alone; her child was not with her.

The good woman was again before the shrine of the Virgin, repeating a last prayer for her dead, preparatory to the painful duties of the morning.

The front window shades were closely drawn to exclude the morning sun, but looking north, to the great, quiet mountains, an open window invited the cool breath of the day.

Without understanding my motives, I took a hasty survey of the silent room. To all appearances everything was as usual.

A sheet had been drawn over the face of the dead, and the holy candles were burning low and pale.

Mariposilla's little cross of white roses was still fresh where the child had placed it, the table of medicines undisturbed except the tumbler containing the unused opiate.

Horrible discovery!

The poisonous glass was gone, and the dark, innocent-looking bottle that remained was empty.

How could I grasp the frightful suspicion? How believe that the Virgin had forgotten her child? How bear the burden of my own selfish slumbers?

Why in the night had I not understood the mocking-birds when they called in vain, "Señora! Señora! Señora?"

A few moments later Arturo bore in his arms from the arbor the lifeless body of Mariposilla.

From her beautiful face the color had faded forever.

We laid her upon her own bed, still robed in the little nightgown, for the long sleep that had closed at last the wakeful eyes.

Poor foolish, beautiful little Butterfly, her summer was now forever ended.

As I performed for the dead girl the last few loving labors, I acquitted her in my inmost heart of her terrible crime. She had meant only to rest, to forget for a time in sleep the anguish of her cruel disappointment.

When from between the great century plants, the yellow edges of their spears shining like avenging swords, passed the hearses—the black one bearing the aged Spanish woman, the white one bearing Mariposilla—I remembered the tragic blooming of the Gold of Ophir rose.

I saw again the old veranda illuminated with Easter glory. I saw timid buds open to full roses. Scintillating in the spring sunshine, more lustrous than all, I saw a child-bud burst into a maiden flower. I saw its petals deepen with the kisses of the sun; then I saw them pale and fall to the ground; for the sun had hidden his face.

I saw the great-hearted Doña Maria bending wearily, as she attempted to gather the scattered petals. I saw the dark Arturo kneel beside her.

Together they seemed to pray; but in the heart of the man was born a horrible curse for those two, now far away.

In my misery I saw the Demon of Selfishness, blacker than night, blacker than death.

I tried to pray—but I could only weep.

THE END

# A Note About the Author

Mary Stewart Daggett (1856–1922) was a beloved American author. After marrying, Daggett and her husband settled in Pasadena, California with their four children. Familiar with the area, Daggett frequently used Southern California as a setting in her work. Having written several novels, plays, short stories, articles, and poems, Daggett was a prolific writer who often explored themes of societal pressure and change, putting human nature under an intimate lens.

# A Note from the Publisher

Spanning many genres, from non-fiction essays to literature classics to children's books and lyric poetry, Mint Edition books showcase the master works of our time in a modern new package. The text is freshly typeset, is clean and easy to read, and features a new note about the author in each volume. Many books also include exclusive new introductory material. Every book boasts a striking new cover, which makes it as appropriate for collecting as it is for gift giving. Mint Edition books are only printed when a reader orders them, so natural resources are not wasted. We're proud that our books are never manufactured in excess and exist only in the exact quantity they need to be read and enjoyed.

# Discover more of your favorite classics with Bookfinity™.

- Track your reading with custom book lists.
- Get great book recommendations for your personalized Reader Type.
- Add reviews for your favorite books.
- AND MUCH MORE!

Visit **bookfinity.com** and take the fun Reader Type quiz to get started.

Enjoy our classic and modern companion pairings!

Printed in the USA
CPSIA information can be obtained
at www.ICGtesting.com
JSHW082358140824
68134JS00020B/2156

9 781513 279152